Sadie was the last woman he'd made love to before his freedom had been ripped away.

And even though he'd hated her for not stepping forward to clear him, while he'd lain on that brick-hard cot every night in prison, he'd fantasized about making love to her again.

Only, now his touch made her cringe with horror.

She wrapped her arms around herself. "You broke in?"

Damn it. He had to be patient. And he had to protect her.

"Because you were screaming," Carter said, intentionally lowering his voice. "I thought the guy who shot at us had broken in." He gestured toward the sheers. "Maybe through the window."

Her gaze darted to the window then back to him, as if she was trying to decide whether to trust him. Whether to believe him.

He suddenly wanted that trust more than anything he'd wanted in a long time.

Almost as much as he wanted his freedom.

RITA HERRON

COWBOY TO THE MAX

TORONTO NEW YORK LONDON
AMSTERDAM PARIS SYDNEY HAMBURG
STOCKHOLM ATHENS TOKYO MILAN MADRID
PRAGUE WARSAW BUDAPEST AUCKLAND

To Ms. Culpepper, my childhood librarian
who taught me to love books.

ISBN-13: 978-0-373-74657-6

COWBOY TO THE MAX

This edition published by arrangement with Harlequin Books S.A.

For questions and comments about the quality of this book please contact us at Customer_eCare@Harlequin.ca.

www.Harlequin.com

Printed in U.S.A.

ABOUT THE AUTHOR

Award-winning author Rita Herron wrote her first book when she was twelve, but didn't think real people grew up to be writers. Now she writes so she doesn't have to get a *real* job. A former kindergarten teacher and workshop leader, she traded her storytelling to kids for writing romance, and now she writes romantic comedies and romantic suspense. She lives in Georgia with her own romance hero and three kids. She loves to hear from readers, so please write her at P.O. Box 921225, Norcross, GA 30092-1225, or visit her website, www.ritaherron.com.

Books by Rita Herron

HARLEQUIN INTRIGUE

861—MYSTERIOUS CIRCUMSTANCES*
892—VOWS OF VENGEANCE*
918—RETURN TO FALCON RIDGE
939—LOOK-ALIKE*
957—FORCE OF THE FALCON
977—JUSTICE FOR A RANGER
1006—ANYTHING FOR HIS SON
1029—UP IN FLAMES*
1043—UNDER HIS SKIN*
1063—IN THE FLESH*
1081—BENEATH THE BADGE
1097—SILENT NIGHT SANCTUARY‡
1115—PLATINUM COWBOY
1132—COLLECTING EVIDENCE
1159—PEEK-A-BOO PROTECTOR
1174—HIS SECRET CHRISTMAS BABY‡
1192—RAWHIDE RANGER
1218—UNBREAKABLE BOND‡
1251—BRANDISHING A CROWN
1284—THE MISSING TWIN†
1290—HER STOLEN SON†
1323—CERTIFIED COWBOY**
1329—COWBOY IN THE EXTREME**
1336—COWBOY TO THE MAX**

*Nighthawk Island
‡Guardian Angel Investigations
†Guardian Angel Investigations: Lost and Found
**Bucking Bronc Lodge

CAST OF CHARACTERS

Carter Flagstone—He is determined to prove he's innocent of the murder he was convicted of, even if he has to force Sadie Whitefeather, the woman who slept with him and then framed him, to help him clear his name.

Sadie Whitefeather—She had her reasons for betraying Carter and is terrified of him and the man who threatened and assaulted her five years ago.

Everett Flagstone—He died of lung cancer after leaving prison—or did he?

Dennis Dyer—Carter was incarcerated for his murder—but was he a pawn in a twisted plan to set up Carter?

Jeff Lester—This brute attacked Sadie and has stalked her for five years; why did he want Carter in prison?

Sheriff Norman Otto—He arrested Carter for murdering Dyer. Is he on the right side of the law or does he have a hidden agenda?

Loretta Swinson—Did Jeff Lester's girlfriend know what he was up to?

Elmore Clement—Carter's cousin inherited Carter's father's land. Only, Carter swears he has no other family. Is Clement a fraud?

Chapter One

Carter Flagstone would die before he would go back to prison.

Which might just happen if he didn't find out who had framed him for murder.

He rolled over on the makeshift bed he'd made in one of the unused barns at the Bucking Bronc Lodge, breathing in the smell of hay, fresh air and freedom.

A freedom that was temporary at best. One that had come at a cost. A guard had been injured in the prison escape, and fingers were pointing at him as the shooter.

His escape only made him look more guilty of that crime and the murder of that man named Dyer, the man he'd been convicted of killing five years ago.

The police had orders to shoot to kill. His damn mug shot was plastered all over the television and in the papers. And if that guard died and the cops caught him, and by chance he *lived,* he'd end up on death row.

Yep, Texas held one of the highest records for executions, and adding his name to the list would be his claim to fame.

Just like his sorry old man's name would have gone on the list if he hadn't developed lung cancer. Hell, the state had decided to save their money and the publicity. Killing a dying man just didn't seem worthy.

His bones creaked and his muscles ached as he unfolded his body from the floor and stood. The scars on his arms and chest looked stark and ugly in the thin stream of light seeping through the slats of the barn.

He'd always been a fighter, but prison had hammered in those instincts and made him better at it. Meaner. Tougher. Harder. Unrelenting.

He would use those skills now to find out who'd framed him, put him in jail and ruined his future.

Then he'd get on with his life.

A desolate emptiness filled him at the thought. *What life?* He'd lost it all the minute the police had slapped the handcuffs on him.

Even before that, he'd been on a downward spiral. He'd had a major rift with his two best friends, who were now rich and owned their own spreads. He'd drunk himself into bar fights and jail more than once before he was incarcerated and earned a reputation that meant no one would hire him if he tried to get a job.

And now his old man was dead, but his ranch had gone belly-up and the bastard hadn't even had the courtesy to will it to him. It was one last dig into his soul that said how much his father had hated him.

Outside, the sounds of the ranch burst to life. The gentle summer breeze fluttering the leaves on the trees. The noise of trucks cranking as workers started the day. The hush of a mare's tail swishing flies.

All sounds he'd missed and yearned for daily. Anything to replace the clank of metal chains, keys unlocking cell doors, feet padding in rhythm as the prisoners were led to the mess hall like cattle to the trough.

Well aware he'd return to that mundane life if he didn't make use of his time, he peeked through the crack in the door to see if the coast was clear. Cows grazed in the lush pastures, two geldings galloped across the flat ranch land, their hooves pounding the grass. The sound of a truck's engine rumbled down the dirt drive.

Maybe it was Frank Dunham, his buddy from the pen who had landed a job at the Bucking Bronc Lodge. Dunham had owed him and helped him hide out here for the past two days, but if the police found out, Dunham's parole would be revoked and he'd go back to jail.

Carter didn't want that on his conscience.

Sweat beaded on his neck as he watched the truck blaze a dusty trail toward the barn. No, not Dunham's. This truck was black, had shiny new chrome wheels, was newer.

He sucked in a breath, his pulse pounding. Twice today he'd seen choppers flying over the property. Had someone caught wind he was here, hiding out like a trapped animal? Had they called the cops?

His ears perked up, listening for a siren.

Then the truck sped past the barn and veered onto the turnoff for the main lodge. Clenching the edge of the barn door with a white-knuckled grip, he watched it disappear in the trail of dust, then finally managed to breathe again.

Another close call. Another reprieve.

It wouldn't last.

The last few days on the run he'd felt the devil breathing down his neck at every turn. The cops. The real killer.

The reality that he was a dead man walking.

Determined and knowing that he couldn't hide out on the Bucking Bronc for long, not with another group of campers due any day now, he unfolded the news article of the fundraiser rodeo Johnny had organized to raise money for the camp and stared at the picture of the woman who could save him.

Sadie Whitefeather.

God, she was beautiful.

Raven-black hair framed her heart-shaped face and delicate features, her high cheekbones accentuating eyes as rich and deep as dark chocolate. Those sinful eyes had mesmerized him, had seduced him. Had made him want to believe that a man like him could not only hold her in his arms but have her.

Those eyes had also held secrets. Pain. A gentle, unspoken understanding that had radiated from her touch.

She had talked of her Navajo ways, her training in medicine with the shaman, her desire to educate herself and become a doctor to help her people. She was also an advocate for the Native American segment and a staunch supporter of environmental issues.

Another seductive quality.

Or so he'd thought.

Dammit. It had all been an act.

She was the reason he'd spent five years in prison, and her day of reckoning had come.

The date on the newspaper proved she'd attended the rodeo a couple of weeks before. Which meant she might be living close by.

For the past two days, he'd been lurking around the ranch hoping she'd show again. Dunham was on the lookout as well, but so far no luck.

His mind rolled back to that fateful night five years ago, and once again he cursed his stupidity. He'd been pissed at his life in general. Mad at his old man for doing an interview from jail, yet again dragging the Flagstone name through the mud.

He'd also had another run-in with Johnny and Brandon. Brandon had beat the hell out of him for sleeping with Kim, his former girlfriend and Johnny's sister. It hadn't mattered to Brandon that he'd broken up with Kim and crushed her heart. That Carter had only tried to comfort her.

Hell, it hadn't mattered to Johnny, either. He'd accused Carter of taking advantage of his sister.

So he'd gone on a drunken tear and ended up at a bar near the reservation. That was where he'd met Sadie Whitefeather.

His body hardened just thinking about her luscious body and the way she'd wound her long legs around him. Her long black hair had hung down her back to her waist, her skin a creamy, sun-kissed Navajo brown, her big, dark eyes haunting and sultry.

One night in her bed and he'd fallen madly in lust.

So he'd gone back for another.

But that night had been his fatal mistake. He'd woken up with no memory of what had happened, with blood on his hands, a dead man on the floor beside him, a man named Dyer who he didn't even know, and the police on his tail.

She had drugged him. That had to be the explanation.

Then she'd disappeared and left him to rot in jail.

He tapped the picture with his finger. Now he'd escaped and he intended to find her. And he would make her talk.

If she didn't, he'd show her firsthand the hard lessons he'd learned in prison, where she had sent him.

SADIE WHITEFEATHER SHIVERED at the news photo of Carter Flagstone as the story of his prison escape and criminal record flashed across the TV screen perched on the wall above the bar.

His dark brown hair was shaggy now, his face unshaven, rough with stubble, his eyes tormented, his strong, stubborn jaw set in anger.

He looked hardened, scarred and lethal.

All deadly to a woman whose dreams of making love to him still taunted her.

Not that he would want her in his bed again.

No, he'd probably kill her.

"Flagstone is considered armed and dangerous," the reporter said. "Police have orders to shoot to kill. If you have any information regarding his whereabouts, please contact the police."

Her fingers itched to make that call. But she didn't know where he was.

Only that he was most likely coming for her.

Of course she couldn't blame him.

What she had done…was wrong.

She sucked in a sharp breath, then rubbed her finger over the prayer beads around her neck. Her mother's people had taught her that all life was sacred. That all things on the earth were alive and connected. That all things alive should be respected.

But she had been a party to a murder and sent an innocent man to prison for it.

Shame clawed at her, but she fought it, struggling with her emotions and reminding herself of the circumstances.

She had had no choice.

The sound of the bell over the doorway tinkled, barely discernible over the wail of the country music floating through the Sawdust Saloon. But her senses were well-honed to detect the sound, knowing it might alert her to trouble.

A cloudy haze of smoke made it difficult to make out the new patron as he entered. He was big, so tall that his hat nearly touched the doorway. And he had shoulders like a linebacker.

He hooked his fingers in his belt loops, standing stock still, his stance intimidating as he scanned the room. Shadows hovered around him, and the scent of danger radiated from him like bad whiskey.

She froze, her heart drumming as she studied his features. Carter?

Or the evil monster she'd been running from for five years?

She hated to be paranoid, but life had come at her hard the night she'd met Carter.

He wasn't the only one with scars.

She had her own to prove it.

Her finger automatically brushed the deep, puckered X carved into her chest, now well hidden by her shirt, and traced a line over it. For a moment, she couldn't move as she waited to see the man's face in the doorway. He was imposing like Carter and her attacker. Muscular. Big-boned. Large hands.

His boots pounded the wood, crushing the peanut shells on the floor as he moved into the light, and her breath whooshed out in relief.

Even in the dim lighting, she could see he had dark-blond hair.

Carter had thick brown hair, so dark it was almost black.

Her attacker—a shaved head, and he'd smelled like sweat and tobacco.

A group of the men in the back room playing pool shouted, toasting with beer mugs, and two men to her right gave her a flirtatious grin and waved at her to join them.

Sadie inwardly cringed, but remembered she needed this job, and threw up a finger gesturing that she would be right there.

"Your order's up!" the bartender yelled to Sadie.

Amber Celton, blond, boobs falling out of the cheap lacy top of her waitress uniform, and a woman who would screw any man in pants, sashayed up beside her and gestured toward the TV screen. "Man, I don't care if that cowboy is armed and dangerous. He could tie me in his bed anytime."

Sadie wiped her hands on her apron and reached for the tray of beer she needed to deliver. Carter had been seductive, all right.

All that thick, scraggly hair. Those deep whiskey-colored eyes that looked tormented, like they were hunting for trouble. That crooked nose that looked as if it had been broken and needed kissing.

And his mouth…thick lips that scowled one minute as if he was the devil himself, then twitched up into a lazy grin that had made her weak in the knees.

And Lord, those big, strong, wide hands. What he could do with those hands was sinful. Downright lethal.

He had destroyed her for wanting another man as a lover.

And her attacker, the one who'd held her down, nearly suffocated her and cut her, he had destroyed her trust in men in general.

"If I were you, I'd stay away from him." Sadie hoisted the beer-laden tray with her right hand, juggling it as she added a basket of peanuts. "Five years in a maximum security prison…you don't know what they did to him inside." Horror stories of beatings and prison rapes tormented her.

"Yeah, but that means five years without conjugal visits," Amber said with a mischievous twinkle in her eye. "I bet he's ready for a woman."

A streak of jealousy pinched Sadie's gut at the thought of Amber taking Carter to bed. Guilt followed that she had helped put him in that godforsaken jail. That five years of his life had been stolen from him when if she'd only told the truth, he wouldn't have been convicted.

Yes. And you would have been dead and so would your mother.

"Hey, sugar, we're thirsty," one of the men yelled.

"And I'm hungry," his buddy shouted, as he reached out a hairy hand to pull her to him. "Hungry for you."

Sadie forced a polite smile as she sidestepped his grip, desperately trying to control a nasty retort that would not only cost her a tip but her job. Five years of working in low-rent restaurants and divey bars just to make ends meet and take care of her mother had taken its toll on her body and shattered her fantasies.

But her mother was gone now, God rest her soul.

Unfortunately so were her dreams of becoming a doctor.

She was broke, alone, and she'd been looking over her shoulder so long that she was half-afraid of her own shadow.

But she had enough sense to know that she was still in danger. Maybe even more so now.

Because Carter Flagstone was most likely looking for her to force her to go to the police about the night of that murder. Which meant the man who'd threatened her life and cut her was probably intent on preventing her from doing just that.

Her own private hell was starting all over.

DARK, HEAVY CLOUDS ROLLED across the night sky as Carter snuffed out the campfire where he'd cooked the fish he'd caught earlier in the stream. He tensed at the sound of a car engine rumbling down the road. He had to hide his tracks.

Still, he was anxious to talk to Dunham and find out if anyone had been snooping around the ranch.

He thought he might have seen something suspicious today. Maybe hints of a cattle rustler. He'd heard they'd had some vandalism and problems before at the BBL, and wondered if this was the same lowlife or a band of rustlers.

Not that he needed to get involved. Hell, no. He had his own problems.

But Johnny and Brandon were dedicated to this ranch, and with more campers due to arrive the next day, they sure as hell didn't need thieves on the land. Especially if they were toting guns.

Most likely, they were.

He rubbed the matchbook with the BBL logo on it, the image of a group of boys getting shot because they'd stumbled on some rustlers, sitting low and heavy in his belly.

The car engine sounded louder, and he stepped

back behind a thicket of trees, gripping his gun to his side as he studied the situation.

Dust spewed in a cloud around the truck, then the muffler made a backfiring sound, and the headlights of a rattletrap truck coasted toward him.

Dunham.

The poor guy's truck was in worse shape than the one Brandon had loaned him.

Relaxing, he shoved the gun in the back of his jeans, but he waited until the truck had parked and Dunham climbed out before he showed himself.

His boots crunched the dry twigs and grass. "Thanks for meeting me."

Dunham gave a clipped nod. "You said you saw trouble?"

Carter explained about the two men he'd seen on the hill in the north pasture. "They had binoculars and looked as if they were staking out the lay of the land."

Dunham made a frustrated sound. "I'll tell Mr. Bloodworth. We'll keep an eye out."

Carter nodded. "How about you? Any sign of Sadie Whitefeather on the ranch?"

Dunham shook his head. "No, man. But I know where you can find her."

Carter's head whipped toward him. Could he finally be this close? "Where?"

"She works at the Sawdust Saloon near the reservation. Cocktail waitress."

Damn. Same job. Different location. And only a few miles from the BBL.

"Did you talk to her?"

Dunham frowned. "Ordered a beer and tried to get friendly, but she brushed me off." He shoved his hands in his pockets. "She's a looker, man. Half the men in the bar were itching to get in her pants, but she wanted none of it."

Carter gritted his teeth. She sure as hell had been receptive to him.

At the time, his ego had soared. He'd been thrilled to have her attention, and her body in his bed.

Little did he know that she'd only been using him. Setting him up to take the fall for murder.

She hadn't been working alone. That much he was sure of. He wanted to know who her partner was. That name would lead him to the killer.

And real freedom. Not this sick shade of it where he was hiding behind shadows and trees, skulking around in the night like a damn snake, afraid to show his face during the day for fear of getting his head blown off.

"Thanks, Dunham, I owe you."

"Just don't get yourself caught." Dunham extended his hand and Carter shook it. "Or killed."

Carter sobered, knowing either one was possible. And could cause Dunham to go back to jail and land Brandon and Johnny in hot water as well for helping him.

"Don't worry," he said. "I'm going to see Miss Whitefeather right now. When I finish with her, she'll talk."

A worried look darkened Dunham's face, but Carter didn't care. He'd spent five long years rotting in prison for a crime he hadn't committed, all because of one night in the sack.

Two, if the one he couldn't remember counted.

Nothing would stop him from making this woman finally tell the truth.

SADIE CLEARED her assigned tables, swept up, then counted her tips. A couple hundred dollars. Hardly worth the never-ending ordeal of fending off dozens of men's wandering hands.

Still, she needed every penny and would add the cash to her medical school fund. If she ever had enough time to study for the MCATS.

She'd barely been able to finish her undergraduate degree for taking care of her mother during her illness. Now...she was so exhausted after work that she couldn't think about studying.

Amber waltzed out the door with one of the men she'd hooked up with for the night, and Big T—Teddy, the owner—waved to her to go on.

Sadie settled her purse tightly over her shoulder, one hand rubbing the leather to make sure her derringer was still tucked inside, then gripped her keys and stepped out the door.

Although questions and doubts needled her. Would she be able to use the gun if she needed to defend herself? Her Native American roots haunted her—every life is sacred…

At one time, she'd been so close to her roots that she hadn't doubted her people's ways. But that was before the attack…

That horrid day had changed everything. Changed *her.*

And she didn't like it.

But she had no idea how to rid herself of the fear that plagued her. Not when it was so real.

Nerves tightening her body, she paused, her gaze scanning the dark parking lot and the corner of the alley, searching to make sure one of the men she'd blown off during her shift wasn't waiting to ambush her. That or the man who'd threatened her years ago. She'd sensed he was following her the last few days.

And now she had to worry about Carter Flagstone.

Stale beer, urine and smoke clogged the air as she rushed to her beat-up sedan. A sound from the alley beyond made her jerk her head around to search again. Something ran across the alley. A stray dog?

Or a man?

Pebbles skittered behind her, then the sound of a garbage lid clanging reverberated through the air.

Anxiety knotted her stomach as she glanced over her shoulder. A homeless man was digging through the trash.

Relieved, she picked up her pace, although the wind lifted her hair and suddenly an eerie premonition skated up her spine.

Someone was watching her.

Adrenaline surged through her, and she ran the rest of the way to her car and jammed the key in the lock. Her hands shook as she opened the door and collapsed inside. She hit the lock, then cranked the engine and tore down the deserted street, her heart ticking double-time as she swung through the alley. She searched left and right, down each side street, over her back to make sure she wasn't being followed. Then suddenly headlights beamed down on her as a truck appeared on her bumper.

Fear nearly choked her, but she forced herself to turn down another side street to throw him off. The truck moved on, and she breathed out in relief, then cut back through another street to her small apartment.

It was in the seedy side of town, but it was all she could afford, and as she climbed from her car, the smell of refuse and body odor assaulted her. Darting a quick glance around to check for predators, she rushed toward her apartment, a corner unit with sagging shutters, mud-streaked siding and unkempt shrubs and weeds shrouding it, casting it in darkness.

Her hand shook again as she jammed the keys in the lock. Then suddenly a hard, cold hand clamped around her mouth, and she felt the tip of a gun barrel at her temple.

"Hello, Sadie," a gruff male voice murmured. "It's time we talk."

Chapter Two

Carter wrapped one hand around Sadie's neck, trapping her in a chokehold as he pushed the gun to her head.

"Scream and I'll shoot."

Her body trembled against his, but he forced himself to ignore the guilt that niggled at him. He'd had plenty of fights with men, but he'd never hurt a woman before.

"Please, don't kill me," she whispered.

He shoved her inside the dark apartment, then slammed the door, needing cover in case someone was watching and called the cops.

A faint glow from a streetlight outside bled through the worn curtains across the room, and he pushed her toward it. "I'm going to release you, but if you scream or try to escape, I will hurt you." He spoke low into her ear. "Do you understand?"

She nodded against him, her fear palpable in the way she dug her fingers into his arm where he gripped her neck.

Carter swung her around and pushed her down onto the threadbare sofa, then aimed the gun at her. The shallow light bathed her face, accentuating the terror in her big, dark eyes. Eyes that had once made him melt.

Eyes that had haunted him since with her cunning lies.

She slid a hand in her purse, and he realized she might be reaching for a weapon. Furious, he straddled her, pinning her down on the sofa as he jerked her purse open. She grunted in pain as his weight bore down on her.

He tried to ignore the feel of her soft, feminine curves beneath his. He hadn't had sex in five years, and her sultry body had been the last one he'd pounded himself into.

Dammit, he wanted her again.

"Get off me," Sadie said tightly.

His fingers connected with cold metal, and he removed a derringer from her purse then dangled it in front of her. "You going to shoot me, Sadie? Framing me for murder wasn't bad enough?"

Emotions flickered across her heart-shaped face, those chocolate eyes brimming with sudden tears. "I'm sorry… I didn't mean to…"

What the hell? Were those real tears? Or was she a consummate actress?

For a moment, he studied her, searching for the

cold-hearted vixen who had seduced him with her lies, then drugged him and hung him out to dry.

But the woman in front of him looked small, vulnerable, even innocent, as if she wouldn't hurt a fly. And she was still so damn beautiful that he felt as if he'd been punched in the chest just like he had the first time he'd seen her in that seedy bar fending off the hands of the jerks who thought her waitress services included servicing them.

She also looked terrified.

She should be, dammit.

Sure, she's terrified. She's finally been caught at her own game.

Hardening himself, he moved off of her, careful to keep his gun trained on her as he stowed hers in his jacket pocket.

"You know I've spent five years in a maximum security prison for a murder I didn't commit, all because of you," Carter said in an icy voice. "You drugged me that night, didn't you?"

She clutched her small-boned hands in her lap, twisting them in the knots of her Navajo print skirt, her face pale and pinched.

"Didn't you?" Carter growled.

Her labored breath rattled out, then she looked up at him and gave a small nod.

Her confirmation made his chest seize with much-needed relief that he wasn't crazy, that he hadn't gone on some drunken rage, killed that man and blacked out and forgotten it.

On the heels of that relief, fury flooded him.

So he had been right. She'd used him.

His hand tightened around the handle of the gun as the memory of waking with all that blood on his hands suffused him. The dingy hotel room, the furniture ripped apart, the tattered clothes strewn about as if an animal had ripped at them.

The jagged hole in the man's chest, the knife in his hand… "Why?"

Another deep breath, and she averted her eyes. "I'm sorry, Carter. I'm so sorry."

"I don't want an apology," he bellowed. "I want the damn truth. Why did you do it? Did someone pay you?" He paced in front of her, waving the weapon, his boots hammering the cheap linoleum. "Did you and the killer plan this, then you picked me out of the bar?" He whirled back around to face her, jabbing his chest with his thumb. "Why, Sadie? Why me? Was I just the biggest fool in the room, or was it because I was falling all over you?"

SADIE WILLED HERSELF to be strong.

Carter had every reason to hate her. But she was terrified he'd unleash five years of rage and kill her.

And as much as she despised herself for what

she'd done, she didn't want to die. "You don't understand," she whispered.

He glared at her with condemning eyes, eyes so cold that he could practically kill with them. His face was rugged, jaw unshaven, the scars he'd gained in jail deeper and puckered.

But beneath the rage, she sensed a wealth of pain, pain she had helped cause by her betrayal.

Where had he been the last few days? Hiding out in ditches? Barns?

All because of her.

The memory of the night they'd made love flashed back. He'd been a bad-boy hellion back then, full of anger, the strong-and-silent type; maybe that was what had attracted her. In bed, he'd been physically demanding, too, had made her body ache with want and desire and need. Yet he'd also been gentle and loving, determined to please her as much as he'd wanted pleasure for himself. And his sexual prowess had been overwhelming.

The gentleness was gone now, though, replaced by a steely intent to exact revenge.

"I asked you—why *me?*" Carter demanded.

She startled at the sound of his booming voice, then forced herself to look up at him. She owed him an explanation.

If it endangered her, then so be it. She was tired of being on the run and smothered by guilt.

"I don't know," Sadie said, clenching her skirt in her hands. "Maybe because you and Dyer had a run-in two nights before."

Carter narrowed his eyes. "We did?"

"You don't remember?" She sighed. "You and he were both drinking, playing pool. It was nothing, just a bar brawl, but I guess the incident made you a patsy."

Carter scrubbed his hand over his beard stubble. "Who were you working with?" Carter asked gruffly.

Sadie's heart thumped with shock. "You have it all wrong," she said, suddenly realizing that Carter thought she had conspired in the murder he'd been arrested for. "I didn't kill that man or have anything to do with it."

Disbelief slashed fierce lines around his chiseled mouth. "You expect me to buy that story? You seduced me, drugged me, then set me up."

"No," Sadie protested, although her protests sounded weak, even to her own ears. The truth was, she *had* helped set him up, even though she hadn't realized it at the time.

He stalked toward her, then jammed the gun in her face again. He was so close she smelled his anger, felt his breath brush her cheek. "Don't lie to me. You owe me the truth, so spill it or you're dead."

Sadie shook her head, her stomach churning. "You're not a killer, Carter. You won't—"

He cocked the trigger. "If you don't think I'm a killer, why the hell didn't you stand up for me in court and say that? Why did you let them lock me up?"

"Because I was scared." Sadie's hand rose to her neck, then unconsciously to the scar on her chest. It ached, the burning sensation triggered by the memory of the man digging a knife in her chest.

Carter's look flattened. "Scared? Scared of what?"

Sadie closed her eyes, willing the memories away, but they consumed her anyway. The big man's beefy hands around her neck, choking her. His rancid breath on her face. His gruff, steely voice rasping threats in her ear.

Suddenly Carter jerked her head back, and her eyes flew open. "Tell me what happened," he growled. "Who set me up?"

Sadie wheezed a breath. "I don't know his name," she whispered. "Just that he broke into my house after you left me in bed that first night we made love."

"The night before the murder?"

She nodded. "He had a knife, he..."

Carter's eyes flickered over her, cold, icy pits of hell. "He what?"

"He put it to my throat. He almost strangled me, then he threatened to kill my mother and me if I didn't do what he said." Her breathing grew ragged. "He knew where I lived, that my mother was sick, and he was going to make her suffer…."

Carter's eyes narrowed to slits as her voice broke, then he swallowed hard, making the vein in his neck bulge. "What exactly did he tell you to do?"

Sadie's heart wrenched. "To slip you a roofie when you came in again." Her voice cracked, tears clogging her throat. "I didn't want to do it, Carter, but I was terrified."

A heartbeat of silence stretched between them, the tension palpable. "Did he tell you why he wanted me drugged?"

"No." Sadie shook her head in denial. "I swear, I had no idea what he was up to. I…thought he planned to rob you or something. It never occurred to me that he was planning a murder."

Carter made a guttural sound in his throat, then stood, moving away as if he could no longer stand the sight of her. Although his gaze remained pinned on her, his look teeming with disbelief, hate and bitterness. "If that's true, then why didn't you come forward once I was arrested?"

The scalding sensation intensified in Sadie's chest, and she rubbed it again. "I told you…I was afraid."

"The police could have protected you," Carter bit out. "And you could have saved me."

The memories flooded her again, trapping her, choking her. "I did try to go to the police," Sadie said, gasping for a breath. "But…but he found me."

Carter gripped her by the arms. "I don't believe you."

Sadie shivered. "It's true."

For a long, silent moment, his eyes bore into hers, then his fingers loosened slightly. "What happened?"

Fury and fear and her own sense of injustice bubbled over, and she unleashed on him. "Because he cornered me in the alley when I was walking to my car. Then he did this."

Her hands shook as she ripped open the top two buttons of her shirt, revealing the hideous scar the man had left between her breasts.

"He held me down…then he carved me up so I wouldn't forget." Tears flowed freely down her face. The cloying smell of her attacker's cheap cologne and sweat haunted her. The sound of his low, wheezy voice echoed in her ears. "He told me the next time he'd kill my mother and make me watch, then he'd finish me off."

CARTER SANK DOWN onto the club chair, his mind struggling to register Sadie's story.

Part of him wanted to deny her claims. Accuse her of lying. Demand she go to the cops, tell the truth and exonerate him.

But her story…her tone sounded so sincere. Riddled with pain and guilt.

And that scar…on her chest. It hadn't been there when he'd slept with her the first time. And he barely remembered crawling in bed with her the second. It was deep and puckered and was only inches from her heart. He'd been in enough knife fights himself to know it had been a serious injury.

All because of him.

His hands shook in front of him as he stared at the gun he'd held on her, and shame filled him. Of all the explanations he'd expected to hear, the excuses, the lies, the cunning act he'd thought she'd put on to save her own life, nothing had prepared him for this.

On the heels of shock, rage choked him. Who in the hell had framed him and terrorized Sadie?

He slowly lifted his head and looked up at her. The anguish in her expression robbed his breath. The instinct to go to her and hold her, to protect her, surged through him. But he needed answers, so he remained rooted to the spot. Still, he couldn't drag his eyes off that X carved on her chest between her breasts.

An X to remind her that the sick bastard was watching and could easily kill her.

Sadie averted her eyes as if she was ashamed, her fingers fumbling clumsily to rebutton her blouse.

Fury that some man had assaulted her and scarred her like that ate at him. The man had obviously wanted to destroy her beauty as well as terrorize her with his threats.

The SOB would not get away with it. If—no, *when* Carter found him, he'd carve him up just as he had done Sadie.

"Who was he?" Carter asked in a thick voice.

Sadie wiped at the tears trickling down her cheeks. "I told you, I don't know."

His gaze shot to hers. "What do you mean, you don't know? You saw his face, didn't you?"

Sadie made a pained sound in her throat. "I… yes, but it was dark. So dark, I'm not sure I would recognize him."

Or maybe she'd blocked it out because of the trauma. "Had you ever seen him before? Maybe in the bar?"

Her small shoulders lifted in a shrug. "I…don't

know. Maybe. But there were men like him in the bar every night. Men pawing at me and watching me. I…tried to ignore them."

He leaned forward, elbows on his knees. "What *do* you remember?"

She sighed, another sound of pain rumbling from her. Then her eyes glazed over, taking on a distant look, as if she was reliving the nightmare. "He was big, almost as tall as you but heavier. And his head was shaved." She bunched her skirt in between her fingers. "He smelled like cheap cologne and sweat and beer."

She was right. That description could fit half the men in Texas, especially at that low-rent bar where she'd been working.

He cleared his throat. "Go on."

She scrubbed at her cheeks as if annoyed with herself for crying. "At first, I was in shock. I… didn't know where to go."

"If you'd called the police, they could have protected you and your mother." And he would never have gone to jail. "And they might have been able to use DNA to track down the bastard who attacked you."

Her eyes flared with derision. "I worked in a bar, Carter. I'm Native American, too. I know how the police work. They would have made me out to be some kind of tramp." She sucked in a sharp breath. "Besides, my mother was dying of cancer. I was all she had. I could barely afford to care for her, much less drag her through a scandal."

"So you just let him get away?" Carter asked, incredulous.

Sadie folded her hands into fists by her sides. "I wanted to come forward, Carter. Believe me, I did. But I told you I was in shock. In fact, the first few weeks after the attack, I was so weak and disoriented I couldn't even get out of bed, much less remember the details of what happened."

A seed of hope burst through the darkness eating Carter's soul. "But you went to the hospital, right? So they have records—"

"I didn't go to the hospital," Sadie said in a low voice.

Disappointment shot through Carter. "No hospital. Why?"

"Because I thought he'd find me there. That he'd kill my mother and then finish me off." She paced to the adjoining kitchen and glanced out the window, her body shuddering as she wrapped her arms around herself. "I didn't know where to turn, so I called a friend from the reservation. He came and took me there to recover, and so the shaman could treat my wound."

Carter cursed, strode to her and swung her around to face him. All this time he'd banked on

Sadie having the answers he needed to clear himself. He couldn't accept the fact that she didn't. "So you're telling me we have nothing. No evidence. That you can't identify this man—"

Her face crumpled. "I'm sorry, Carter. I—"

Something rattled outside, jerking his attention, and he threw up a finger to shush her. She tensed, her eyes widening, as he peered through the window at the alley.

A shadow moved across the glass pane then suddenly something crashed through the window where they were standing.

Sadie screamed. Carter jerked her down to the floor as glass sprayed the counter and carpet.

Suddenly smoke began to billow through the room, stinging his eyes and throat.

Dammit. It was a pipe bomb.

Whoever had set it off wanted to kill them.

Chapter Three

Sadie dove down beside Carter, coughing as thick smoke clouded the room. "My God, what's happening?"

"It's a pipe bomb. Come on, we have to get outside." Carter grabbed her hand. "Stay behind me and keep low." He wielded his gun as if he was ready to shoot, then tugged her toward the kitchen and the back door.

Sadie grabbed her shoulder bag on the way out, her heart racing. The man who'd attacked her... He knew Carter had escaped. He'd been following her.

All those shadows the past few days, the sensation of someone watching her, of someone breathing down her neck...it had been real.

He had come back to kill her, to kill them both....

Carter pushed open the back door and she ducked behind him, clinging to his hand as they stepped onto the tiny cement patio. She struggled to inhale a breath, desperate to escape the smoke, and rubbed her beads, murmuring a Navajo prayer for her and Carter's safety.

When she opened her eyes, though, the air smelled rancid and dank, and the alley was dark and filled with more shadows.

"Come on," Carter whispered.

The sweltering heat plastered Sadie's hair to her skin and clothes as Carter tugged her around the corner of a dilapidated brick building. She nearly stumbled over a pile of garbage someone had thrown in the street, and clung to Carter to keep from falling.

"Where are we going?" she asked, her lungs churning for air.

"My truck. It's down the street."

Suddenly the sound of gunfire rent the air. A bullet whizzed by their heads, and Sadie screamed again.

"Dammit, he was waiting." Carter yanked her behind the corner of the building. "It was a setup to lure us out of the house."

"Do you see him?" Sadie asked.

"No."

She scanned the black corners of the alley, trembling as she watched Carter lift his gun and peer around the edge of the building. Voices echoed from somewhere down the street. An engine rumbled. Tires screeched.

She followed Carter's gaze, checking the tops of the buildings nearby, the back entrance to the deserted warehouse two doors down, the corner of the street across from them.

Two cars were parked on the curb. The first, a dented green Ford that belonged to the junkie in the apartment next to her. The other, a silver Jeep that had been abandoned days ago and had been stripped, hubcaps and all.

Another shot pinged off the concrete wall by Carter's head, and he pressed his back against the building to dodge it, then pushed her head lower. "Stay here. I'll see if I can draw him out."

Panic streaked through Sadie, and she clutched his arm. "No, don't go, Carter. He might kill you."

Carter swung his gaze back to her, seemingly startled that she might care. "I'll be fine, Sadie. Just stay here."

"No." She held on to him like a lifeline. "We're in this together."

He narrowed his eyes a fraction, doubt darkening the hues of his eyes, then gave a quick nod. "All right. Let's make a run for my truck." He gripped her arm with his hand. "But promise me, if I get hit, you'll go to the police and tell them everything."

Fear closed her throat. “Don’t talk like that. You aren’t going to get hit.”

“Promise me,” Carter said. “If you can’t make it to the police, call Johnny Long or Brandon Woodstock. They’ll protect you and help clear my name.”

Sadie nodded, although it terrified her to admit that they might not make it out alive. But if Carter did get killed, she would need help. She couldn’t keep running scared for the rest of her life.

And without Carter, it was only a matter of time before she ended up dead.

CARTER REFUSED TO DIE in this damn alley. And he would not let Sadie become a victim to this low-life.

Not again.

He sucked in a sharp breath, then pulled Sadie behind him, keeping low as he crept along the edge of the buildings. Pulse jumping, he searched the alley and streets, his senses honed. Where the hell was the shooter?

A trash can lid rattled, then rolled across the alley ahead. Footsteps clattered and a shadow moved. A flash of something metal caught in the darkness and drew his eyes toward the roof of the run-down apartment building next to Sadie’s.

The shooter. Was he up there? Watching? Taking aim?

His mind raced. The pipe bomb had been thrown into the house from the main level. So if this cretin was on the roof, he had a partner.

Another bullet pinged off the metal awning above his head.

"Dammit, this guy is pissing me off," Carter growled. He turned and fired back at the direction the shot had come from. Not the roof but from behind the Jeep.

His truck was a few more feet away. "Come on." He yanked Sadie around the corner then cut through another alley in between the warehouses.

A mangy dog pawed at a garbage can, knocked it on its side and began to scrounge through the trash. Voices rumbled from inside the next building, and through the foggy cracked window, he spotted two men. A drug deal going down.

They glanced up, both scowling, mean looking and armed. One headed toward the door as if he thought they might be cops, and Carter picked up his pace, dragging Sadie behind.

Another bullet pinged toward them just as he reached the truck. He shoved Sadie down behind the bumper, jostled his keys from his pocket, opened the driver's door then coaxed Sadie inside.

"Get down on the floor!" Carter shouted, as he spotted the shooter leaving his hiding spot behind the Jeep to chase them. Another bullet shattered the front windshield, spraying glass as Carter jumped inside. He ducked again to avoid being hit, punched the gas and tore from the curb.

His tires squealed as he raced down the street, and he swerved from side to side to throw off the shooter.

But the sound of another shot bouncing off the truck bed echoed behind him. He glanced in the rearview mirror hoping to see what the man looked like, but he wore a black face mask, black jacket, black clothes.

Only the shiny metal of his automatic weapon gleamed in the darkness.

SADIE CROUCHED LOW, her stomach lurching as Carter spun the truck down the road. The sound of the bullet pinging off the back made her cover her head, and the glass on the floor was digging into her knees.

Carter screeched and swerved to the right in a fast turn. Car horns blared, and another vehicle's tires squealed as if the car was about to hit it. She braced herself, but Carter must have managed to miss the collision, then he whipped the truck around onto the highway. For the next few minutes, she closed her eyes and prayed as he wove back and forth through town, then she heard the hum of other traffic and realized he'd turned onto the main road.

"I think it's safe. You can get up now," he said in a gruff tone.

Sadie was shaking all over. The truck cab swirled as she lifted her head and looked up at him. His jaw was clenched in anger, the beard stubble making him appear rough and dangerous. So did the feral look on his face.

"Where is he?" she said in a raspy whisper.

"I think we lost him." He reached his hand out to help her up, and Sadie stared at it for a moment, unsure if she was ready to completely trust him.

Regret flared in his eyes. "For God's sake, Sadie. I'm not going to hurt you." He lowered his hand and brushed glass from the seat. "If I'd wanted to, I would have back there at the house."

But he had threatened her. And he hated her.

Still, he was all the protection she had, and he *had* saved her life. So she slowly pulled herself from her shock and climbed in the seat.

"Buckle up," Carter said. "For all I know he had a partner waiting to ambush us."

Sadie nodded and hooked her seat belt, then leaned her head back, her body racked with tension.

"Did you get a look at him?" Carter asked.

She shook her head. "No, did you?"

"Not his face. He was a big guy, dressed in all black. Wore a face mask."

"It has to be the same man who threatened me," Sadie said. "The last few days I sensed someone was following me."

Carter jerked his head toward her. "You mean since I escaped?"

She clenched her hands together. "Yes. I thought it might be you."

Carter worked his mouth from side to side. "He probably figured I'd come after you to find out the truth."

"Because I was the only one who could clear you," Sadie said, the guilt once again suffocating her.

"Right. And of course, I played right into his hands." He shot her a dark look. "That means he won't stop until he kills both of us."

A shudder rippled up Sadie's spine, and she turned to stare through the window. Clouds gathered in an ominous gray haze, obliterating the stars. A quarter moon hung low in the Texas sky, the dim glow casting shadows across the cacti, scrub brush and mesquites dotting the wilderness.

Carter steered the truck to the right onto a dusty road, and in spite of the heat Sadie suddenly felt a chill as she realized they were heading out into the country where it would be deserted.

And they would be alone.

She hadn't been alone with a man in five years.

BITTERNESS AND THE NEED for revenge fueled Carter's temper. Sadie had helped ruin his life.

But she'd been tortured and threatened to keep her from going to the police on his behalf.

Had the killer targeted him personally because he had a grudge against Carter? Or had he simply been an easy mark because of his drinking?

Sadie's breathing rattled in the silence, and she rubbed that scar. Anguish rolled through him. The night they'd made love he'd actually thought he'd felt something special with her.

Then everything had gone wrong.

And now she was afraid of him. That was obvious.

Not that he could blame her. Hell, he was a convicted felon. He'd served five years in prison with murderers and rapists and other hardened criminals. He'd tangled with plenty of them in fistfights and knife fights, and spent time in solitary confinement.

And he had held her at gunpoint.

"Where are we going?" she asked, her voice trembling.

"Some place to lay low for a while."

Her eyes widened, her fear a palpable force vibrating in the air between them.

Suddenly aware he was practically kidnapping her, he glanced over his shoulder to make sure they weren't being followed. But they'd left the town and civilization behind. Making a snap decision, he swerved off the road, careened to a stop and faced Sadie.

She gasped and clenched her arms around her body as if to protect herself. A mixture of emotions slammed into him again. For God's sake, she thought he was going to attack her.

Shame washed over him. It had been so long since he'd dealt with anybody but criminals and prison guards who'd treated him like an animal that he'd forgotten how to be human. Gentle.

Reining in his temper, he held up his hand to indicate he didn't intend to accost her. "I'm sorry about tonight. Is there someplace you'd like to go? Someone you trust to keep you safe?"

Surprise flickered across Sadie's face, then she seemed to relax slightly. Still, she twisted her skirt in her fingers. "No. There's no place."

"Don't you have family?"

She shook her head. "No. My mother died last year."

She looked so small and lost and vulnerable that his chest clenched. He wanted to pull her in his arms and comfort her.

But the moment he lifted a hand toward her, she shrank like a delicate flower wilting in the sun.

He gritted his teeth, silently cursing the past and the circumstances that had led them to this point.

"How about a friend?" he asked, intentionally lowering his voice. "Someone at the reservation?"

Her eyes widened, pits of steel. "I can't endanger them, Carter. This man has kept track of me for five years. He knows you're out, and now that he's seen us together, he's not going to give up until he silences us." She heaved a weary sigh. "And he'll hurt anyone we care about to get to us."

Carter grimaced, hating that she was right. He'd long ago learned to stop living on empty hopes and senseless fantasies that people were good. No…most of the time they stabbed you in the back.

He pinched the bridge of his nose, struggling to formulate a plan, but his head ached from trying to figure out his next move. He was a cowboy, not a cop or the devious criminal everyone had pegged him to be.

But he had to think like one if he was going to survive and clear himself.

Having Sadie with him would make it more difficult to hide out. Then again, the police were looking for him, not a man and a woman, so it might serve to his advantage to travel as a couple.

Although if the police discovered they were together, they could arrest Sadie for aiding and abetting a convicted felon.

But what choice did they have? If he left her alone and that jerk found her, no telling what he'd do to her this time before he killed her.

And he *would* kill her.

Dammit. He had enough guilt to last a lifetime. He couldn't live with Sadie's death on his conscience.

SADIE STRUGGLED to quell the fear raging inside her as Carter started the engine and pulled back onto the road.

She had once been a strong woman. She was an advocate for the Native American community, had fought for her people and their rights. She had studied the Navajo way of medicine, learned the roots and herbs used to help treat illnesses, the prayers and rituals performed to help with the healing of the body, the mind and the soul.

But she had also seen such poverty and backward ways that she had wanted more for her people. She had excelled in school because her education was her ticket out of poverty. She had set her sights on medical school in an effort to bridge the gap between the reservation and the surrounding areas in terms of medical care.

Then her mother had been diagnosed with cancer.

And she'd been forced to take waitressing jobs to pay medical bills and hire a nurse to tend to her mother while she worked. It had been a vicious cycle that had left her drained, and with no time to study, she'd lost her scholarship and her dreams.

Then Carter had walked in that night with his sexy, bad-boy swagger and talked her into his bed, and she'd fallen into his arms. She'd even imagined a relationship beyond the bedroom. A life. A future.

But then she'd been attacked…

Nausea roiled through her. For five years, she'd run from that memory. From the hulking monster who had threatened her and abused her and left her scarred both physically and emotionally.

She wouldn't run anymore.

Carter had been unjustly accused and incarcerated. But she'd lived in a prison of her own, as well.

A prison built on fear.

Carter deserved justice. And so did she.

Together they would find the truth and go to the police. And if she died trying to do the right thing, at least she'd go to her grave with a clear conscience.

Exhausted, she closed her eyes and let the rumble of the truck eating the miles lull her into sleep. She had no idea what time it was when they jolted to a stop, but when she opened her eyes, they were at a deserted ranch in the middle of nowhere.

A thread of anxiety knotted her stomach, but Carter was scowling as he looked across the property, and he didn't appear to have sex on his mind.

Instead his face was contorted with pain.

"Where are we?" she asked.

"My old man's ranch," Carter muttered.

"Is he here?"

Carter shook his head. "SOB died a few weeks ago. Place is run-down, but we can hide here for the night."

"Won't the police be watching it?" Sadie asked.

Carter shrugged. "Maybe. But Brandon said they've already searched it once."

Anger laced his voice, but Sadie decided not to push for more information. Still, as he pulled the truck into a sagging barn, then climbed out and shut the barn door to hide the truck, she realized how isolated they were.

If Carter had been lying about protecting her, he could kill her and dump her out here, and no one would ever find her.

Irritated at herself for losing ground with her resolve to be stronger, she opened the door and slid down from the truck seat. Carter still had her derringer. She had to get it back.

At least with a gun in her hand she might have a chance at protecting herself from Carter. Or from the man who'd stolen her life and her sanity for the past five years with his constant threats.

Her mind warred with her Navajo beliefs, but she had to stand her ground. This man was evil, had scarred her and had destroyed too many lives.

She'd kill him before she allowed him to touch her again.

CARTER SCANNED THE PROPERTY, in case someone had followed them, then grabbed his duffel bag and led Sadie into the house. He hadn't seen the place in years, and the shabby, run-down conditions were worse than he'd expected.

At one time, he'd had lofty dreams like Johnny and Brandon. He'd known one day his old man would get locked up or killed by someone he pissed off, and he'd thought this land would be his. He'd planned to bring in cattle, some horses, work it from the ground up and have something to be proud of.

Hell, he didn't even care if he was rich like his buddies. He just wanted something of his own. A piece of land. Freedom. To earn a respectable living.

To be able to walk the streets without people calling him a murderer.

Bitterness welled inside him at the irony that

he'd hated his old man and his violent tendencies but that he'd ended up in jail just like him.

And when his old man had been released from prison, he'd come back to the ranch to live out his last days. Had he hoped Carter would show up so he could pound his fists into him one more time before he died?

Or had the bastard mellowed?

A sardonic chuckled bubbled in his throat, riddled with disgust. No, his father hadn't had a decent bone in his body.

And judging from the peeling paint, rotting porch, cobwebs and dirt streaking the farmhouse, he hadn't done anything to improve the place once he was released. Of course, he *had* been dying...

Served him right for all the pain he'd inflicted on others.

Sadie tried to flick on a light, but the bulb popped. Hell, he was surprised the power was still on at all.

"I know it's a rattrap," Carter said. "But at least we can get some rest and regroup in the morning."

Sadie nodded, and he showed her up the stairs to one of the bedrooms. The faded blue paint of his little brother's room had turned a dingy gray, dust coating the old dresser and iron bed in the corner.

"Was this your room?" Sadie asked, as she

glanced at a yellowed poster of a country rock group taped on the wall.

"No, it was my brother's."

"Where's he now?" Sadie asked.

Carter swallowed hard. "He killed himself. Couldn't take my old man anymore." *And I had already cut out and deserted him.*

The familiar guilt plowed through him. He should have taken his brother with him.

Sadie gave him a sympathetic look, but he didn't deserve it. Besides, she looked dead on her feet. Realizing they'd left her place with no time for her to pack anything, he unzipped his duffel bag, yanked out a denim shirt and tossed it to her. "Here, you can sleep in that. Now get some rest. If you need anything, I'll be down the hall."

She worried her lower lip with her teeth. "Carter?"

He turned to go, but paused at the sound of her voice. "Yeah?"

"Can I have my gun back?"

He studied her for a long moment, then his gaze fell to her trembling hands, and he removed it from his jacket and laid it on the nightstand. "Just don't shoot me with it, okay?"

Relief softened her face. She'd probably slept with that gun since her attack. He understood about the demons that emerged at night and wished he'd had a damn gun in prison.

"I won't," she said in a strained voice. But a small smile curved her mouth, reminding him of how beautiful she was, and lust hit him hard.

Dammit, he had to leave or he'd haul her up against him.

What in God's name was wrong with him? Every night in jail on his cot, he'd thought of her, remembered her seductive eyes and body. Remembered the soft curve of her breast, the dusky ripe brown of her nipples, the creamy skin of her hips, the damp invitation between her thighs…

Then he'd start sweating and shaking and wake up nearly howling like an animal. Because he remembered how she'd used him.

For five years, he'd considered her his enemy.

But now, he suddenly wanted to protect her and make love to her again.

He was damn crazy.

Hadn't prison taught him he couldn't trust anyone?

He balled his hands into fists and strode down the steps, his boots pounding out his frustration on the rickety wooden steps. Hell, yeah, it had.

He had escaped for one reason and one reason only. To clear himself. Not to get laid or hook back up with the woman who'd put him in jail.

He'd keep them both alive long enough to find the real killer, then they'd part ways.

Steeling himself, he stopped at the bottom of the stairs. He heard the door close and lock upstairs, and a bitter laugh escaped him.

Why the hell would Sadie or any woman want to be with him anyway? He had nothing to offer.

His boots clicked as he strode through the downstairs searching for more weapons. He found a shotgun and rifle and carried them back up the stairs and down the hall toward his old room. Tomorrow he had to make a plan. Figure out a way to find the man who'd framed him.

But it was late and his adrenaline had waned, so he yanked off his clothes and fell onto the metal bed he used to call his, wearing only his boxers.

Even though he was worn out, he couldn't sleep for the troubling memories crashing down on him. Memories of things that had happened in this house. A house that had been filled with daily horrors.

The brutal tongue-lashings. The physical beatings. The night his old man had broken Carter's nose when he'd thrown him against the wall.

The day when he was ten and his father had stripped his clothes, tied him to a tree and beaten him with a switch until his legs had been bloody.

His brother had been terrified and had hidden in the woods.

Brandon and Johnny had found him, untied him and carried him to the creek to clean his wounds. He'd been half unconscious, spitting blood and feeling humiliated.

But both of them had admitted that their daddies were just as mean, their houses just as sick and twisted, then they'd shown him their scars. The moment had bound the men together forever.

Carter had vowed to stand by them after that, and the three of them had protected each other.

Another memory splintered through the haze, this one even more painful. The day his daddy had killed his mother.

Carter had run away as fast as his legs could carry him.

He shouldn't have been so selfish. Should have taken his brother with him.

But his brother had been the golden boy, the one his father loved. It hadn't occurred to him that his father would vent his rage on him.

And in the end, he hadn't had to. His brother had killed himself.

And here he was back in the same crummy house he'd started in. Only his life had gone to hell. He had a criminal record, the law on his tail and a man who was determined to kill him breathing down his neck.

He racked his brain trying to recall an image of the man Sadie said he'd fought with in the bar, but those days and nights he'd been in an alcohol-induced blur, and nothing registered.

Disgusted, he closed his eyes and finally collapsed into a fitful sleep. But sometime later, a noise jarred him awake.

A car? Footsteps? He scrubbed his hand over his face, disoriented.

Then a scream pierced the air. A scream that cut through the chilling silence. Sadie's scream.

Had the damn bastard found them?

He grabbed his gun from the dresser, yanked his jeans on, although he didn't take time to snap them, then raced down the hall.

He had to get to Sadie.

Chapter Four

Carter raced down the hall, wielding his gun, his senses honed for trouble. He hesitated at the door to the room where Sadie slept and cocked his head listening for…the sound of a man inside? Footsteps? A man's voice?

"No, stop…please," Sadie cried. Then a thrashing sound and something hit the floor. A lamp?

A second later, another bloodcurdling scream pierced the air. This one was filled with pain and terror.

He jiggled the door, but it was still locked. How the hell had the man gotten in?

His heart drummed with panic, and he slammed his body against the wooden frame. The thin, rotting wood splintered, and he braced himself and hit it again with all his weight, so hard his shoulder wrenched.

He didn't care, though. He had to get inside.

The force of the impact cracked the edging and the door burst open. Darkness bathed the room, but his gaze flew to the bed where Sadie was thrashing. A tiny sliver of moonlight sliced through the ratty sheers and broke the darkness, allowing him just enough visibility to search for the predator.

But the window was closed. The room empty, except for Sadie.

Pulsing with sweat, he blew out a relieved breath as he realized she was in the throes of a nightmare.

Shoving his gun into his waistband, he scanned the room again then jerked open the closet door just to make certain an intruder wasn't hiding inside.

"Stop, please, no..."

Sadie's tormented cry wrenched his gut, and he shot a quick glance below the bed, confirming there was no one underneath. Then he lowered himself onto the mattress beside her and reached out a hand to wake her.

"Sadie, honey, wake up," he murmured. "You're dreaming. You're safe now."

"No, don't." She threw up her hands and fists and hit him, obviously trying to fend off her attacker.

He gritted his teeth at the sight of her half naked in his shirt, willing his libido in check as the edges gaped open. His gaze fell to the puckered scar at the center of her chest, and he cursed.

She was reliving that night she'd been attacked....

Damn that bastard.

She kicked him, her ragged breathing punctuating the silence. His throat thickening, he stroked her arm and reminded himself he had to treat her with kid gloves. She was terrified and had been abused.

"Sadie," he said softly.

A guttural sound tore through the air as she shoved at the covers. Then she shifted sideways and lunged upward as if she was going to run. She made it halfway off the bed when he caught her by both arms and pulled her to him. Her body was trembling, her breathing labored, her hands clammy as she gripped his arms.

"Shh, you're okay, you're safe, I'm here with you."

She tried to jerk away again, but he shook her gently. "Wake up, Sadie. It's me, Carter."

She stopped thrashing momentarily as his voice registered, although her body went stone still. He cradled her face between his hands, determined to break her out of the terror gripping her. "You're just having a nightmare."

Sadie's eyes flicked open, and she stared at him

with a glazed look, as if she had no idea where she was or what was happening.

But the terror in her face at the sight of him made his gut tighten.

"Let me go," she said in a voice so haunted that he released her immediately.

He held his hands up indicating he meant her no harm, but she shuddered anyway. "I'm not going to hurt you, Sadie. You were screaming, having a bad dream."

She glanced down at her nightshirt where it gaped open at the top, then at the splintered door where he'd broken it and shock settled across her features. "I'm sorry I…woke you."

His gaze locked with hers. "No problem. I'm a light sleeper." He shrugged. "A habit I picked up in prison. Always had to be alert."

Pain drew her face into a frown, then her gaze lifted to his scarred cheek. Self-consciously he rubbed a finger across it. He'd never considered himself a handsome guy, but before prison he hadn't been hideous, either. At least he hadn't scared little children and old women.

"Ugly, I know."

"I guess we both have scars," she said softly. "They've changed us."

"Maybe." But she was still the most beautiful woman he'd ever met.

Her tender voice stirred memories of the first time he'd laid eyes on her. She had been wearing a turquoise-and-red Navajo skirt with a red blouse and sandals, her black hair hanging in a long braid down her back, turquoise earrings dangling from her earlobes. The other men in the bar had all been ogling her, muttering obscene comments, talking dirty.

He had wanted to knock their teeth out.

Because he'd wanted her for himself. But not just because he knew she'd be the hottest sex he'd ever had.

There had been something more to her. A deep, reserved, quiet kind of beauty that had triggered his lust but also his admiration. She wasn't like the other girls he'd known in high school, snotty and materialistic, women who'd looked down on him as the trailer-trash troublemaker.

No, Sadie had looked at him as if she saw something *good* in him. As if she saw beneath his hard surface to the man he wanted to be.

He cleared his throat, the memory of having her in his bed returning to taunt him. He had loved her with his mouth and hands and body once and brought her to ecstasy. In fact, she had screamed with pleasure.

And he had moaned her name as he'd come inside her.

He balled his hands into fists. She was the last woman he'd made love to before his freedom had been ripped away. And even though he'd hated her for not stepping forward to clear him, as he'd lain on that brick-hard cot every night in prison he'd fantasized about making love to her again.

Only now his touch made her cringe with horror.

She wrapped her arms around herself, jerking her nightshirt tightly to her, then glanced at the table where her derringer lay. "You broke in?"

Frustration slammed into Carter. But the image of that scar flashed in his mind, and he knew Sadie deserved to be skeptical.

Dammit. He had to be patient. And he had to protect her.

"Because you were screaming," Carter said, intentionally lowering his voice. "I thought the guy who shot at us had broken in." He gestured toward the sheers. "Maybe through the window."

Her gaze darted to the window then back to him, her big, dark eyes searching his face as if she was trying to decide whether to trust him. Whether to believe him.

He suddenly wanted that trust more than anything he'd wanted in a long time.

Almost as much as he wanted his damn freedom.

He shifted and leaned against the doorjamb. But

he'd waited five long years to clear his name. And nothing was going to stop him from doing so.

Even Sadie Whitefeather.

SADIE SHRANK BACK against the headboard, needing more distance between her and Carter.

Her heart was pounding so loudly she could hear it roaring in her ears.

Having Carter in the bedroom close enough to touch her, close enough to breathe in his masculine scent, felt too intimate for comfort, and it reminded her that she hadn't been with a man in five years.

And he had been practically naked. God, the man was sexy. But that sex appeal scared her now, too.

Carter might have spent those years in a cell, but in some ways she'd locked herself in a self-imposed prison of her own. She'd been afraid to get close to anyone, had avoided men, especially physical relationships, and had hidden herself away, as if staying invisible and holding on to her secret could keep her alive and assuage her guilt.

But she hadn't really been living. No, she'd grieved for her mother, berated herself for her lack of courage, tormented herself with images of the beatings and abuse Carter suffered in prison, and spent each day running in fear.

"I'm sorry," Sadie said again. "I…thought the nightmares were over, but—"

"But my escape brought them back," Carter said in a self-deprecating tone.

"It's not your fault," Sadie admitted. Suddenly weary, she buried her head in her hands. "You've been locked up for a crime you didn't commit, and I've been running from city to city, hiding, trying to lose myself, trying to forget."

"But you couldn't forget," he said bluntly.

She shook her head, tears burning the backs of her eyelids. Tears she refused to let fall. She didn't deserve his sympathy. "No matter where I moved, the truth—and that man—followed me."

Carter cleared his throat. "Where did you go?"

The last few years of running replayed through her mind. She'd hated the hiding, the lying, the not being able to trust or make friends. "After my mother died, I moved to Houston for a while. Then Dallas. Then Austin. Each time I thought I might be able to escape the bad dreams. The guilt…" Her voice cracked, and she looked up at him with her heart in her eyes. "The guilt over what I did to you."

The sound of Carter's breath rasped in the tense silence that followed. He scrubbed his hand over the back of his neck and sighed. "Sadie, don't—"

"I hated myself," Sadie said softly. "But I was

too scared. Every time I'd get up my nerve to come back, I'd sense someone following me. And then there were the notes. They came every few months."

"Notes?" Carter asked.

Sadie nodded. "Notes to remind me to keep silent. Sometimes they'd show up in the mail. Sometimes I'd find one stuck in my purse or on my car window. Sometimes one would be delivered with a gift."

"What did the notes say?"

"That he knew where I was. That he was watching. That I could run but I couldn't hide."

Carter crossed his arms, a vein throbbing in his neck. "What about the gifts?"

"Usually photographs." She pulled the edge of the blanket up over her legs, suddenly feeling naked and exposed. "Candid shots of me at work, at my apartment, working in my garden, getting in my car, taking a walk—"

"To let you know that he was close by." Carter cursed. "The damn bastard has been stalking you."

Sadie nodded, and Carter lowered himself onto the mattress facing her. She tensed, then forced herself not to shrink away like a terrified animal. But Carter's strong masculine scent and body filled the space and made her pulse pound with fear.

And desire.

A desire that she hadn't felt in years, a desire that she'd never expected to feel again.

Then he reached for her hands. Her stomach clenched, and she sucked in a sharp breath.

"I'm sorry he hurt you," Carter said gruffly. He splayed his big hands in his lap as if to prove he didn't plan to maul her. "It's my fault you're involved in all this."

Sadie jerked her gaze to his. Taking blame for her attack was something she'd never expected to hear from Carter. Instinctively, she sensed the turmoil eating at him now just as she had years ago.

He was broken; he had been for a long time.

She ached to comfort him, to fix him. But she was too broken to do anything but try to survive herself.

No, you're not. You're stronger than that. You stood up for your people on the reservation. You've managed to live in a world between the reservation and the white people.

You can stand up for yourself now.

Emotions welled in her throat. "It's not your fault, either," Sadie whispered hoarsely.

They sat for a long moment, the strained silence ticking with the truth that they had both been used, were both victims. The need to reach out and touch Carter crawled through Sadie, but she could not bring herself to follow through.

Finally Carter sighed, a world-weary sound that tore at her. "Maybe not. But we're here now and I can't go back to jail."

Sadie's lungs squeezed for air. She'd seen the news, knew that the police considered Carter armed and dangerous. He was a wanted felon.

Grasping for the last remnants of the courage she'd once possessed, she forced her hand to move toward his. An inch, another, then she inhaled sharply and covered his splayed hand with hers.

"Then we have to stick together and track down the real killer," she said, working to make her voice strong. "I don't intend to live the rest of my life on the run, terrified, looking over my shoulder."

Carter's gaze locked with hers, a myriad of emotions playing across his rugged, scarred face. She tried to read them and saw worry, anger, bitterness and frustration. Then something softer, more gentle, something she dared not analyze.

In the next second, she recognized hunger and had the insane urge to crawl into his arms and beg him to hold her. To protect her.

To assuage the pain of the past.

To give herself to him the way she had five years ago and show him that he was lovable.

But her chest throbbed as the memory of her attacker's knife boring into her chest resurfaced, and she released his hand and folded her arms, once again cloaking herself inside her silent prison.

Together they would find this man and see that justice was served.

But that was all that could ever be between them.

CARTER FELT THE WEIGHT of his hatred for Sadie lifting, the aching bitterness that had eaten at him for the endless months of his confinement shifting on to the man who had assaulted, threatened and stalked her.

The jerk had not only planned the murder, suggesting premeditation, but he had orchestrated a devious plan to cover his tracks and framed him for the crime.

Questions once again plagued him. Why him? Had the setup been personal, or had he simply been an easy pawn because of his own stupid, angry, drunken bouts?

"You're right. This guy has to pay for what he did to both of us."

Sadie nodded, looking stronger now she'd made her statement.

He stood, brushing his hands down his jeans,

suddenly realizing he hadn't snapped them and his zipper was riding down.

Sadie's gaze shifted to his crotch, and his sex hardened. Her eyes widened, then she jerked her gaze to her hands and he backed toward the door.

"I'm going to see if my old man left a computer here," Carter said. "Maybe if I study the notes about my trial and Dyer, I can find a lead as to who killed him."

Sadie tucked a strand of hair behind one delicate ear. The braid was gone now, the locks draping her shoulders. He wanted to run his fingers through them.

She backed away from him. "I'll see if I can find something for us to eat."

Carter yanked his zipper up and snapped his jeans, willing his erection to dissipate. Being around Sadie was going to test that situation. It might become a permanent problem.

So he turned and hurried from the room, strode to his bedroom and yanked on a T-shirt, then headed down the stairs to his father's office.

His father had never been much for organization, but the office looked as if it had been ransacked. Either that or his father had turned into one of those hoarders like he'd seen on TV from his cellblock. Papers, magazines, old newspapers and bills littered the battered oak desk, floor, filing cabinet and coffee table, which was situated by the faded leather recliner his father had lived in when Carter was little. How many times had he climbed in that chair when his father was passed out and imagined beating on him the way the old man had beaten on him?

Cigarette burns and scratches marred the ancient wood floor, and the scent of must and mildew clogged the air. Layers of dust coated the rusty brown curtains that had been hanging for decades, and years of stale beer spilled on the floor and chair lingered like the acrid odor of a dead animal.

Using his handkerchief, Carter wiped his face, then inhaled several deep breaths, willing the stench of the past to abate so he could focus.

He didn't give a damn about his old man. Carter was only here to hide out long enough to dig up some information.

He shoved aside mountains of papers and found an old laptop beneath a stack of bills that had been stamped Overdue. One letter threatening foreclosure drew his eye, and he bit the inside of his cheek with anger.

If he'd been free, he would have worked his butt off to save the ranch. Now...his life was in the toilet and the land was about to go to the bank.

And he would be left with nothing.

Shaking his head at yet another injustice, he reminded himself that the ranch was not a priority. If he didn't clear his name, he would either spend his life hiding out on the run, go back to prison or…end up six feet under.

With everyone thinking that he'd died a murderer.

Determination set in, and he sank into the rolling desk chair, checked the computer and plugged it in, then booted it up. The old machine whirred and spit out noises that made him wonder if it actually worked, then he checked to see if there was Internet access. No wireless, but there was a modem.

Ancient, but it would have to do until he had access to something better.

He spent the next few minutes reviewing a depressing preview of the articles covering his arrest and trial. God, if he didn't know he was innocent, he would believe the press and lawyers himself.

They had paraded his past in front of the jury, highlighting every detail of his trailer-trash life, from his scraps as a youth, to the night his mother died, then to his days as a juvenile when he'd purged his anger in brawls with whoever was close by.

Then his brother, Rick, had killed himself.

The video feed from the bar the night he'd

tangled with Dyer portrayed him as a two-bit loser cowboy with serious anger issues, cementing the DA's case and significantly maligning his character.

He rubbed his hand over his forehead, then forced himself to ignore the bitterness building inside him. He had been out of control back then. He had fought with Dyer.

Had woken up with blood on his hands. His prints on the murder weapon. And he'd had no memory of what he'd done.

But he hadn't killed Dyer.

Not that he hadn't doubted himself at first.

But during his incarceration, snippets of his memory had returned in flashes that felt so real he'd realized he was reliving actual events. That he hadn't killed that man in cold blood as the cops had claimed.

He just had to prove his innocence.

He looked up Dyer on Google, then skimmed information on the man he supposedly killed. Dyer had worked construction and odd jobs. He'd also been in trouble with the law himself.

The sound of Sadie entering the room made him jerk his head up. She was dressed in the same skirt and blouse she'd worn the night before. Damn. No more peeks at her legs beneath his shirt.

The scent of coffee wafted toward him and he noticed two mugs in her hands.

"I found some coffee in the cabinet," she said quietly. "I don't know how old it is, but I made a pot anyway."

"Trust me, Sadie," Carter said, his stomach rumbling. "I've had worse."

She nodded, cradling her cup in her hand. "Did you find anything?"

He shrugged. "All the old articles about the trial. Now I'm researching Dyer."

"The man you were accused of killing?"

"Yeah." He clicked another article detailing one of Dyer's arrests, and Sadie moved closer, peering over his shoulder as a photograph of the dead man appeared.

Sadie's sharp gasp rattled in the air. "Oh, my God."

Carter swung his gaze toward her. Her olive skin had faded to a pasty shade. "What's wrong?"

Sadie pointed to the photo, a picture of a beefy man in handcuffs next to Dyer.

"That's the man who threatened me."

Chapter Five

Sadie shivered, her eyes glued to the photograph of the man who had threatened her, carved up her chest and stalked her.

Granted, it had been dark that night, and the shadows in the alley and his black clothing made it difficult to see his face. But for a moment when he'd thrown her against the wall, pressed his heavy body against hers and dug the knife into her flesh, she had looked into his face.

But she'd blocked out the memory.

The image flashed in her mind now with vivid clarity, as if he was standing in front of her again.

The rough, unshaven jaw. The bulbous nose. The jagged front tooth that had been broken. The leering look.

The mole above his left eye.

His body odor, the scent of his sweat and the cigarette dangling from his crooked mouth, the intense aroma of bad beer—the rancid smells swirled around her in a dizzying rush.

She staggered slightly, and Carter stood and gathered her against him. “Sadie, are you okay?”

“I thought I’d forgotten what he looked like, but…it all just rushed back.”

“You were probably in shock,” Carter said gruffly.

She made a sound of disgust in her throat. “But that’s him. I can…still smell him.” And feel the rough bristles on his jaw as he’d scraped his face against hers and whispered threats in her ear.

Carter stroked her back with his hand, rubbing slow circles to soothe her, and she took several calming breaths the way the shaman at the reservation had taught her to do after the attack.

“Sit down,” Carter murmured. “I know this is difficult, Sadie, but identifying him will help us find him.”

She didn’t know if she wanted to find him. To face him…

Carter helped her into the chair, and she fidgeted with the beads around her neck while he scrolled down the page.

“Son of a bitch’s name is Jeff Lester. He was arrested nine years ago for assault and battery. Served four years, then was released on parole a few weeks before Dyer was murdered.”

Sadie rocked back in the chair, desperately trying to remain calm when her heart was beating so fast she thought it might explode in her chest.

"Dyer worked construction and odd jobs," Carter continued. "He and Lester were arrested together, but Dyer never served time. Apparently the charges against him were dismissed on some technicality."

"I don't understand," Sadie said, struggling to put the pieces together. "You think Lester killed Dyer?"

Carter shrugged. "I don't know, but they are connected, and it's the only lead we have." He pulled a hand down his chin, then scrolled to another article about a scam the two men had been accused of. "Looks like they might have been involved in some crooked deal together. But Lester went to jail, and if they had made money scamming people, Dyer might have taken off with the cash. Then Lester got out of jail and tried to recoup his loss."

Sadie twined her fingers together. "That sounds feasible."

"It's just a theory." Carter rapped his knuckles on the desk. "Unfortunately we have no proof."

"If Lester was on parole, he'd have to check in with a parole officer."

Carter arched a brow. "Right." He tapped some keys, then researched several other sites featuring stories of arrests, criminal records, any links to Lester that appeared, until he discovered a story about a parole officer named Wade Lungston. Lester had been listed as one of his parolees.

"Dammit," Carter said, then highlighted the story for Sadie to read.

Her pulse clamored as she skimmed the piece. "Lungston died in a suspicious accident."

Carter grimaced. "What you want to bet it was no accident? That Lester murdered him?"

Sadie shuddered. "But Lester was never arrested for the crime."

"He would have been assigned a new parole officer." Carter searched for more information. "Apparently all the parolees were questioned in the death." He sighed in frustration. "Lester had an alibi."

"People lie," Sadie said matter-of-factly.

Carter nodded. "Yeah. And in the case of Dyer's death, the cops had me in custody, so they didn't look any further. They just locked me up and closed the case."

"It's not closed." Sadie injected confidence into her voice. "We'll find out the truth and clear your name, Carter."

Carter's chiseled face tensed with concern. "Even if you have to confront Lester?"

Sadie shuddered again, but forced her chin up,

finally allowing her anger to override her fear. "Yes, Carter. If it's the only way we'll both be safe again, I'll confront him."

After all, Lester had used her mother's life to force her into keeping silent, but her mother was gone now, and she was alone.

Jeff Lester had robbed five years from both her and Carter. And if he found her, he'd kill her. It was time for her to stand up to him and take charge of her own destiny.

And it was time to get justice for Carter.

That meant Lester had to pay.

CARTER WANTED TO DENY Sadie's statement, but she was right. Lester was already on their tail. If they didn't find him and expose his criminal actions, he'd wind up killing both of them.

Sadie sipped her coffee then stood. "There wasn't much in the pantry, but I did find a couple of canned goods that haven't expired. I'll heat them up."

"Thanks." Carter gritted his teeth, grateful she wasn't running from him this morning. "I'll see what else I can dig up on Lester. If I can find the name of the person who gave Lester his alibi, maybe we can break his story. At least that will be something to give to the police if we're caught."

Sadie took another look at the photo of Lester, her dark eyes tormented, then she set her jaw as if gathering courage before she left the room. Admiration for her stirred deep in his gut.

He had immediately been drawn to her when he'd met her at the bar because of her exotic looks and sensuality.

And in prison, he'd hated her for her betrayal.

Now he knew the truth—that she had suffered as much as he had, that she had her own nightmares chasing her—he wanted to make it up to her for involving her in this mess.

If he hadn't picked her up at the bar, Lester wouldn't have threatened her to get to him.

He skimmed through two more articles until he discovered the information he needed. The name of Lester's alibi. A woman named Loretta Swinson.

Knowing he needed help, he punched in Johnny's number. Johnny had hired a P.I. for him before. Unfortunately the man had been murdered working his case.

Maybe Johnny knew another private investigator who could help.

Johnny answered on the third ring. "Brandon?"

"No, it's me, Carter," Carter said. "I'm using a phone Brandon gave me."

"Good God, Carter, where the hell are you?"

Carter ran a hand through his hair. "It's better

you don't know," Carter said. "I don't want to incriminate you and Brandon."

"Dammit, Carter, it's always been the three of us watching each other's backs. Nothing's changed."

Emotions thickened Carter's throat. "Yeah, but—"

"But nothing," Johnny continued. "Brandon and Kim and I care about you. The last thing we want is to see the police put a bullet in you."

Johnny's words bolstered Carter's resolve. "I have to clear myself," Carter said, although he knew Johnny and Brandon couldn't possibly understand his need for revenge.

Not just for himself, but now for Sadie.

Johnny muttered a string of expletives that could blister paint, then sighed heavily. "All right. What can I do to help?"

Carter explained about Sadie and Jeff Lester. "He's been stalking her, threatening her, and he set me up," Carter said. "I think he killed Dyer."

"Sounds plausible," Johnny said. "But you said he had an alibi."

"Yeah, some woman named Loretta Swinson. I need to find out where she is and talk to her."

"I'll call the P.I. I used when Lucy was kidnapped," Johnny said. "Maybe he can locate her."

"See if he can get an address for Lester, too. He

may or may not be staying in one place, but there might be something there to help the case."

"Got it." A tense pause followed. "Carter?"

Carter pinched the bridge of his nose, his friend's voice reminding him of all he'd lost, and the rift that had nearly shattered their friendship. "Yeah?"

"Be careful, man," Johnny said gruffly. "I don't want to bury you. I want to see you come home."

Carter chuckled. Johnny always had a flair with words. "That's the plan."

He disconnected, then stood and stretched and went to find Sadie. Staying at the Flagstone farm was a nice reprieve, but it wouldn't last long.

Even though the police had already searched it, they could come back any minute.

He and Sadie had to be ready to run when they did.

SADIE HAD ALWAYS USED cooking to distract herself from problems.

Although nothing could totally make her forget her situation. Her mother had taught her how to make fresh corn cakes and cook over an open fire. She'd also shown her which herbs and plants to pick for healing potions and home remedies.

Now she wished she had access to that garden and the fresh herbs. Instead the cupboards were bare and she was hoping the bugs and rats hadn't contaminated the little cornmeal left.

The fact that she was scrounging around in the cabinets of Carter's father's deserted farmhouse for food, listening for the sound of a police siren, and jumping at every screech of the wind or noise outside for fear it was Jeff Lester, drilled home the danger dogging her.

And that the man in the room next to her was wanted for murder.

An innocent man who stirred up primal feelings she could not allow herself to act upon.

Trembling at the reminder of his hands rubbing her back, she dumped cornmeal in the bowl and checked it for bugs, relieved that it appeared clean. Then she added water and stirred it to make a dough that she pressed into a thin tortilla. It wouldn't be the best-tasting one she'd ever made, but it would help fill their stomachs. She fried the thin, flat shells, then opened the cans of corn, black beans and tomatoes she'd discovered in the pantry and filled the tortillas. Cilantro and spices and cheese would have made them better, but she had to work with what was here, and that wasn't much.

She'd survived on less, though. And Carter's comment about prison implied that he had, too.

By the time she'd heated the tortillas, Carter appeared, his coffee mug empty. "It smells good."

Sadie shrugged. "It would have been better with fresh ingredients—"

"Hell, Sadie," Carter said with a chuckle. "I've been eating prison slop for years. And we're on the run. I didn't expect you to cook for me, much less whip up a gourmet meal."

A sharp pang stabbed at Sadie.

He deserved better.

His black T-shirt strained against the broad expanse of his chest as he settled down in the hard wooden chair. She poured him another cup of coffee, and his fingers brushed hers as she handed it to him. Their eyes locked.

A tingling sensation fluttered in her belly at the contact, the air around him breathing with masculinity. He looked like a renegade, dangerous and sexy, one that made her feel alive and yearn to be touched.

"Thanks, Sadie," he said in a gruff tone. "I...I'm sorry you got caught up in this mess."

Aching to touch him, Sadie offered him a tentative smile. "Let's just concentrate on staying alive long enough to expose Jeff Lester for the slimeball he is."

Carter grinned, reminding her of the brooding, sexy man she'd met in the bar that night. He was the roughest, toughest-looking cowboy she'd ever laid eyes on, and she had wanted him with a fierceness that had obliterated her good sense.

Now his cheekbones were more hollow, almost gaunt, and scarred, the darkness in his eyes telling horror stories that she wasn't sure she even wanted to hear.

A heartbeat of silence stretched between them, then he turned to his food and wolfed it down. Sadie joined him with another cup of coffee and managed to eat a few bites herself, although her stomach churned with nerves.

"I talked to my friend Johnny," Carter said, using the back of his hand to wipe his mouth. "He hired a P.I. to help me a while back."

Hope rallied in Sadie's chest. "What did he find?"

Carter's look darkened. "He was murdered."

Sadie choked on the coffee, coughing and spilling it on her hand. The hot liquid scalded her fingers, and Carter immediately reached for her and coaxed her to the sink. He turned on the cold water and held her fingers beneath it to soften the sting.

Sadie sucked air through her teeth to control the fear and panic. "Because he was looking for me?"

Carter's feral gaze locked with hers. "I think so."

Guilt assaulted her. How many people had to die to cover up Lester's devious plan?

Her mind whirled with random pieces of the past few weeks. "Is that the reason you escaped?"

"One of them." Carter lifted her hand to examine the burn and Sadie's heart melted. He was so tender and seemed so concerned, yet she'd heard about the escape, that he had almost killed a guard.

"I didn't plan the escape," Carter said as if he had read her mind. "Two other prisoners did. But when that bus broke down and one of them uncuffed me, I had to go for it. I had to prove who framed me and killed the P.I. trying to help me or I'd die in prison and no one would ever know the truth."

She started to pull her hand away, but Carter tightened his hold. "Sadie, I don't know what you heard, but I didn't shoot that guard. I tried to stop the other prisoner from killing him."

Sadie's chest heaved for air, and this time she did pull her hand from Carter's. She wanted to believe and trust him. She wanted him to hold her and assure her everything was going to be all right.

But she'd seen too much evil in her life to believe that lie.

Neither of them might come out of this alive.

CARTER SEARCHED SADIE'S FACE, desperate for her to believe him. The entire world might think he was a damn liar, a cold-blooded, calculated murderer, but he didn't want Sadie to think badly of him.

He wanted her to look at him the way she had when they'd first met—as if she could see beneath the surface of his bad-boy exterior and find the good man inside.

Suddenly the sound of a helicopter broke the silence, and his heart slammed against his ribs. Damn.

Sadie must have heard it, too, because her eyes widened, and she ran to the window and looked out. Carter slipped up behind her, peeled back the ratty curtain and studied the sky.

The rumbling sound grew louder, and he glanced to the east and spotted the bird soaring above the trees. Was it just a chopper on a routine trip to another part of Texas?

Or had the cops found them?

SADIE'S STOMACH PLUMMETED. She zeroed in on the side of the helicopter as it coasted over the tops of the trees coming closer. There wasn't a logo, although it could be an undercover cop. Or Lester…

"Is it a police chopper?" Sadie asked.

Carter grabbed her hand. "We're not waiting around to find out. Come on, we have to get out of here."

"Where are we going?" Sadie asked.

"I don't know, but we can't let them find us." He dragged her through the kitchen, then paused at the back door and peeked outside through the foggy glass. He scanned both ways, and she clenched his hand, her heart pounding as she scanned the distance and listened for a police siren.

Instead, the whir of the helicopter grew louder.

"Stay low and let's run for it." He pulled her out the door and they crouched low, hugging the side of the house until they reached the edge. Then he gestured toward the barn where they'd hidden the truck, and they raced toward it. Carter opened the barn door, and she ran behind him and climbed in the truck.

"Duck down," he ordered as he slammed his door and started the engine.

Sadie did as he said, trembling as he floored the engine and headed down the dirt road that wound through the property. Tall oaks, pines and mesquites swirled past, the truck bouncing over ruts and ridges in the gravel.

Seconds later, he swerved onto another side road that was even bumpier.

"Where are we going?" Sadie asked.

"There's an old shack that's torn down on the

south end of the ranch and a mine. We'll hide out there."

Sadie braced herself as the truck ground the dirt and rocks, then looked up at the sun slanting through the window. It was daylight. The chopper could easily spot them.

"Did he see us?"

"I'm afraid so," Carter said. "He turned this way."

Fear clawed at Sadie. They couldn't get caught now.

Carter swung the truck over a hill, then soared downward. The impact threw Sadie against the passenger-side door. Her shoulder slammed into it with such force that she had to stifle a moan, then he screeched to a stop.

When she sat up, she realized he'd sandwiched the truck between a cluster of mesquites. He climbed out and hurriedly plucked rotting pieces of wood from the torn-down shack and spread it around the truck. She jumped out and grabbed brush and limbs from the area and covered it.

The chopper roared closer, but Carter yanked her down a small incline, then dropped to his knees. "Come on."

She fell to the ground and crawled inside the mine, trembling as the stench of a dead animal wafted around her. Her hands brushed over dirt and pebbles, then moss.

It was so dark she couldn't see, though, and Carter paused to touch her hand. "We'll hide in the corner behind that ledge."

Sadie shivered as the cold emptiness of the interior engulfed her, and Carter led her into the darkness. They dropped to their knees and crawled along the ledge toward an indentation that had been carved from the stone walls, then burrowed back inside the narrow space behind an overhang of jagged rocks. The smell of wet, rotting moss permeated the air, and the edges of the stones were slick with moisture. Somewhere nearby she heard the trickle of water and wondered if there was an underground source, or if the cave had once been used for mining.

The sound of a bat screeching or maybe a rat cut into the silence, and Sadie searched the shadows, biting her lip to keep from crying out in revulsion.

Outside the sound of the helicopter zooming lower made her clench Carter's arm.

"Be very quiet," he whispered. "If they touch down, they'll probably search the area."

Nerves clawed at Sadie as he pulled her up

against him, and she buried her head into his arms and prayed whoever it was didn't find them.

She didn't want to die or for them to go to jail, either.

Chapter Six

Carter wrapped his arms around Sadie, his heart hammering at the way she buried her head against him. He sensed her fear because it mirrored his own.

"Do you think it's Lester?" Sadie asked.

"It's hard to tell," Carter said. "I doubt Lester owns a chopper."

"But what if he's not working alone?" Sadie suggested. "What if someone else hired him to do their dirty work?"

"Good point." Carter pulled her closer. "You know, Sadie, you could go to the police and tell them what happened," he murmured. "They could protect you."

"Maybe, maybe not." She clung to his arms. "For all I know, they wouldn't believe me. They might think I was working with Lester, just like they thought you were."

True. "At least if they had you in custody, you'd be safe."

"Would I?" Sadie pulled back to look at him. Her eyes were luminous pools, filled with turmoil and worry, and so damn beautiful that his heart stuttered. "You and I both know that if Lester wants me, he'll find a way to track me down, no matter where I am."

He couldn't deny that possibility. Lester probably had friends on the inside and out, ones he could pay to come after her. And if Lester hadn't killed Dyer, and the investigation led to a conspirator or something bigger, they might have more to worry about than Lester.

The roar of the helicopter cut him off from saying more, and she burrowed her head into his arms again as they listened to it dip lower. It zoomed along above them, dipping up then down between the pockets of trees, then the hum intensified, the sound indicating they were hovering, studying the area. Carter tightened his grip on her, moving them back as far into the crevice as possible. The drip, drip, drip of water punctuated the eerie silence, and wet moss dampened his back.

Carter held his breath as the chopper set down, and kept his eyes trained on the entrance of the cave as he and Sadie waited.

If the police found them, he'd go back and rot in jail. If they didn't kill him first.

And what would happen to Sadie? Would the

police believe her story and investigate? Or would they arrest her for aiding and abetting a wanted felon?

Seconds ticked by, dragging into agonizing minutes as they listened to the sounds outside. The blades of the chopper cutting through the air. Voices of men as they combed the woods. Pebbles skittered as someone crawled inside the cave. A flashlight panned the interior cutting across the stone walls and floor and sweeping toward the side of the mine where they were hiding. Footsteps echoed as the man paced the interior, searching.

The flashlight beam sliced the darkness near them, and Carter dropped his head against Sadie, his heart thundering as the man slanted the rays over the ledge. He held his body rigid, forcing himself to lie still, to shield Sadie, to muffle her soft gasp of fear with his body as she trembled against him.

A loud sigh punctuated the air. Feet moving.

"Damn, they're not here."

"I thought you saw something," a second man said.

"It must have been a deer."

"No sign of a vehicle?"

"No. I guess if he was here, he didn't ditch it like I thought."

"Probably made it to the highway."

"It was a truck, right?"

"Yeah. Dark color. Pretty beat up." The man mumbled a sound of frustration. "We'll do a search for stolen pick-ups. Maybe we'll get a pop."

"Let's go back to the house. If he was there, maybe he left something that will tell us where he's going next."

The other man released a sinister chuckle. "Then we'll trap him."

SADIE FINALLY RELEASED a breath as the sound of the men's voices faded outside.

Carter squeezed her hand. "As soon as the chopper leaves, we need to make a run for it."

"But what if one of them stayed behind to set a trap?"

Carter hissed between his teeth. "That's a chance we'll have to take. We can't stay here or they might come back."

Sadie nodded against him, thankful for his quiet strength. The next few minutes the strain took its toll. Sadie's body ached from lying still, her pulse clamored from being so close to Carter, and she began to feel claustrophobic, the darkness closing in around her. Images of the night in the alley when Lester attacked her came flooding back, but she forced herself to block them out, and reminded herself that Carter was holding her now, not the man who'd cut her.

Outside the wind picked up, the rumble of the chopper's engine blasting the tense silence. Somewhere nearby Sadie heard another sound—a hissing sound.

Not Carter this time.

"Carter, it sounds like a rattlesnake—"

He tensed, his grip growing firmer. "Shh, I know. It's behind me on the wall."

"Shoot it," Sadie whispered.

"No, someone might hear." He slowly released her and gestured for her to crawl away from the ledge. Sadie held her breath again as she eased herself away from him. But she immediately felt bereft at losing the physical contact.

"I'm right behind you," he said gruffly.

Sadie moved slowly, dragging herself along the cold dirt flooring. Suddenly the rattler's hiss screamed in the silence, and Carter swung around and slammed a rock on the ground.

"Is it dead?" Sadie asked.

"Yeah. Let's go." He grabbed her hand and they raced toward the entrance. When they reached the narrow entryway, they both dropped down again, and he gestured for her to let him go first.

Carter removed his gun from his jacket and wielded it in front of him as he crept through the opening. Sadie swallowed hard as she followed him.

She just prayed no one was outside waiting.

CARTER PULLED SADIE behind him, weaving between the mesquites and cypresses until they reached the truck. Together they removed the limbs and rotting wood they'd used to hide the vehicle, then he unpocketed the keys, they jumped in and he gunned the engine.

He turned left, heading away from the direction the chopper had flown and his father's farmhouse, took one of the dirt roads leading east, checking his rearview mirror to make sure no one was following.

Sadie fastened her seat belt, the air between them vibrating with tension.

"Were they cops?" Sadie asked.

Carter shrugged. "I don't know. Could have been, or they might have been working with Lester."

"I don't understand what's going on," Sadie said. "I assumed Lester killed Dyer and framed you, but you think there might be someone else involved."

"It's hard to say." Carter noticed a car zooming up the road behind them and swerved onto another side road that wove through the wilderness.

Cacti, scrub brush and dilapidated buildings that had once been inhabited but now were falling apart dotted the landscape. The air felt hot, thick, muggy, the Texas sun climbing ruthlessly in the sky like a ball of fire that sucked the life from the land.

The car raced closer, and he clenched the steering wheel with a white-knuckled grip. Sadie whirled around and held on to the seat. "He's gaining on us."

Carter floored the truck, but it was old and rattled with the force of the accelerated speed. Seconds later, the car closed in on them, nipping at his tail. He glanced at the rearview mirror, expecting to see blue lights swirling and to hear a siren, but suddenly the car's gears ground and the driver swerved the car around and flew past them.

"Thank God," Sadie whispered, as it disappeared down the road in a cloud of dust.

Yeah. Thank God. But they weren't home free.

In fact, they needed another place to hide until Johnny located Loretta Swinson. Hopefully she held the key to finding Lester.

His mouth felt dry, and a headache pulsed behind his eyes. He wished to hell he'd thought to pack provisions in the truck, at least some water, and made a mental note to stock up when they spotted a store.

Wiping at the perspiration on his forehead, he checked the gas gauge. They had less than half a tank, and he'd driven this road enough times to know that they wouldn't find a gas station for miles, maybe not until the next small town.

Unless someone had built a gas station while he was incarcerated. But judging from the desolate emptiness of the land around them, he doubted it.

He kept his gaze peeled for trouble as the truck ate the next sixty-five miles. Sadie remained silent, seemingly lost in her own world, probably wishing she'd never met him. Her life would have been normal, she'd be safe, she wouldn't have suffered the trauma of Lester's attack…and she wouldn't be running from the cops and a madman now.

Guilt once again weighed on his chest. If he hadn't been drinking that night…

Stop it, he told himself. Recounting his past mistakes wouldn't help now. Finding Lester and clearing his name was the only way to make things right.

And he wanted to make them right for Sadie now as much as he did for himself.

Finally signs for a small no-name town appeared. They were still an hour from Laredo, but they needed gas and to take a breather.

He swung onto the paved road, noticed a red station wagon ahead then glanced up to see an SUV and a van coming up behind them. Forcing himself not to panic, he slowed his speed, filing into traffic so as not to draw attention to them.

"There's a sign for a discount store ahead," Sadie said. "Maybe we should go inside and look for some kind of disguise."

"That's not a bad idea."

Sadie chewed on her bottom lip. "We should probably change vehicles at some point, too."

Carter frowned, a muscle ticking in his jaw. "You sound like you've done this before."

Sadie sighed. "I've been running ever since the attack."

Carter's throat clogged with a mixture of anger and remorse. He knew he should keep his distance from Sadie, but he couldn't help himself. He reached out and drew her hand into his. "I promise you we'll end this, Sadie, and you won't have to run the rest of your life."

"Neither will you," Sadie said softly. "We just have to solve the murder so you can clear your name."

Her voice held such conviction that he latched on to hope. For the first time in years, he actually felt like someone believed in him, that his future might hold something other than life in that eight-by-ten cell.

An eighteen-wheeler raced toward them, a police car on its tail. The policeman slowed and cut his gaze toward Carter, and Carter took a deep breath and forced himself not to react.

But his pulse hammered. Had the police discovered he was driving Brandon's truck?

Hell, he'd have to ditch it and steal another mode of transportation. But that was a last resort. And stealing a car would add another crime to his list.

Then again, he was a lifer. What could be worse?

Suddenly the police car spun around, its siren blaring, and raced back toward them. Carter's palms began to sweat.

Dammit. If the cop caught them, it would be over before he had a chance to prove his innocence.

SADIE HELD HER BREATH as the police car sped up, its siren blaring. The officer cut around the sedan two cars back, then the SUV behind them and coasted up on their tail. He was going to stop them. Then Carter would be arrested and hauled away, and she'd either go to jail or be left on her own to deal with Lester.

A roadside vegetable stand that had long since been abandoned appeared to the right, then a turnoff heading back toward the major highway. Carter swerved onto it, obviously hoping to lose the cop.

But the police car turned as well, and Carter gripped the steering wheel and started to veer to the side of the road. The police car vaulted forward after him, but suddenly a red sports car flew past them.

The policeman hit the gas and chased after the speeding car, leaving Sadie and Carter behind.

"I can't believe it," Carter said. "I thought he had us."

"Me, too." Sadie plucked at a loose thread on the hem of her blouse. "All the more reason for us to find some new transportation and disguise ourselves."

Carter nodded, and they fell into a strained silence, both alert in case the policeman decided to send another cop after them. Finally, a half hour later, they breathed easier and stopped at a gas station.

Sadie used the ladies' room while Carter gassed up. She picked up a couple of bottles of water and some snacks, her gaze landing on the newspaper by the counter as she stopped to pay.

The front-page article featured a story about the prison break and the convicts still on the loose. She grimaced at Carter's mug shot, then glanced around and noticed the clerk behind the register had a copy of the paper by the cash register. He was looking out the window, squinting at Carter as if he was trying to determine whether he was the face in the news.

"Excuse me." Sadie set the water and snacks on the counter. "I'd like to pay for these." She grabbed a paper and laid it beside the other items.

"You with that man in the truck?" the clerk asked.

"Sure thing. That's my husband, Roger. We left the kids with my folks so we could take a little second honeymoon." Sadie pasted on a smile and patted her stomach. "We needed a little time to ourselves before baby number three comes along."

The pimple-faced kid studied her for a moment, then grinned and began to ring up her purchases. Sadie paid for them, then smiled again, her nerves on edge as he glanced at the paper once more.

The urge to run hit her, but that would only draw suspicion, so she gave a little wave, then grabbed the water and snacks and sauntered out the door.

But as soon as she reached the truck, she glanced back to see if the clerk was watching. He was, and he had a phone to his ear.

"We have to get out of here," Sadie said. "I think that kid in the store recognized you from the paper. He may be calling the police."

Chapter Seven

Carter clenched his jaw, started the engine and pulled back on the road, careful not to speed away or attract any unwanted attention. "Damn. Did the clerk say anything?"

"He asked if I was with you. I told him we were married and left the kids with my folks while we went on a second honeymoon."

He arched a brow, a glint in his eyes. "You covered for me?"

"For us." Sadie shrugged. "I had to do something to throw him off."

Us? Carter hadn't been a part of a couple in so long he didn't know how to respond.

He studied Sadie for a long moment, emotions swirling in his chest as his gaze caught the dark hues of her eyes, then dipped to her high cheekbones and those delicate lips that curled upward when she smiled and slashed into a straight line when she was mad or determined.

She looked determined now.

She'd been fiercely loyal to her mother, had sacrificed her career to care for her when she was sick, and now she was standing up for him.

He didn't deserve it.

He was a felon on the run.

If the cops discovered Sadie was helping him, they could arrest her, too.

He had to keep her with him to protect her. But in the end, he'd make sure the police knew she was innocent.

He jerked his gaze back to the road, the haunting memory of his first night in jail gnawing at his gut. When the doors on that cell had clanged shut, and he'd realized he wasn't going to be released, he'd felt so alone and hopeless he'd wanted to die.

He'd vented that frustration and fear out on his two best friends by blaming them for not giving him an alibi.

For not *lying* to save his sorry butt.

But he'd been wrong to lash out at them. Johnny and Brandon had been like brothers, and he'd virtually cut them off in spite of his desperate need for their support at the time.

But now they'd halfway forgiven him and were helping him try to clear his name.

And so was Sadie.

A car horn honked, jerking his attention back to the road and the situation, and he tried to pull himself together when emotions welled in his throat. Emotions he had to control.

He didn't like being vulnerable.

He'd learned to be tough growing up, and prison had drilled in the need to stay that way. He couldn't go soft on Sadie.

Hell, no. She was only staying with him because Lester wanted her dead.

As soon as he cleared himself and they put Lester away, she would go her own way, and so would he.

He couldn't grow attached to her or fantasize about a future for the two of them.

He'd given up thinking anyone could love him a long damn time ago.

SADIE FROWNED at Carter's sudden silence. She didn't know what she'd said that had upset him, but she sensed his withdrawal as if he had erected a physical barrier between them.

She knotted her hands together, then unknotted them and toyed with the Indian beads around her neck, silently murmuring a Navajo prayer as she struggled for inner peace and balance.

She had only been trying to help.

For the next half hour she lapsed into her own world, focusing on the future she wanted. Life on the reservation had been difficult for her and her mother, but Sadie had always been drawn to nature, to the herbs and plants and gardens. She had loved animals as a child and had a tender side for them as well as humans. And she'd been infatuated with the shaman, with the prayer rituals and healing ceremonies of her people.

She had studied the Navajo culture as a teenager, yet she'd also witnessed the poverty and ignorance—rather, stubbornness—of some of her people in accepting modern medicine. She'd wanted to know both the traditional Navajo cures and the newest, most modern medical treatments, as well. She'd respected both, and had planned to go to medical school to bridge that gap between the two worlds.

The sight of a falcon flying across the sky, its long wings splayed as it gracefully coasted over desert land, reminded her of all she loved about her people and fortified her strength.

She would finish medical school and accomplish what she'd set out to do. And nothing, especially Lester, would stop her.

Her resolve intact, she relaxed, watching the scenery pass in a blur and appreciating nature. But soon the wilderness gave way to signs of the city as they reached the outskirts of Laredo.

Laredo was so close to Mexico that it was a prime spot for criminals to cross the border.

Had Carter considered escaping into Mexico and disappearing forever?

It didn't sound like a bad idea at the moment.

But then she would never be a doctor. She'd be deserting her people and her dreams. And Carter's name would never be cleared.

She glanced at his stubborn jaw and stony eyes and sensed he wanted that as much as he wanted his freedom. As much as she wanted her medical degree.

Running would not accomplish either.

She spotted a sign for a discount store. "Look, Carter, let's stop there. We can buy some clothes to disguise ourselves."

Carter gave a clipped nod, then swung into the parking lot, checking the periphery for police as he shifted the truck in to park. When he stopped, he removed his hat and scrubbed his hand through his hair, spiking the long strands and sending it into disarray.

His labored sigh sounded tired and weary. She wanted to reach out and comfort him. To watch over him for a night so he could sleep without the nightmares that dogged him constantly.

The sun was beginning to peak in the sky, the oranges and yellows casting a sheen of light across the roof of the store and parking lot.

The heat was blazing, the temperature near a

hundred with no relief in sight. Seconds after the air conditioner flicked off, perspiration dampened her forehead, her shirt sticking to her skin with the cloying heat.

He reached for his wallet, pulled out a small wad of bills and started counting his cash.

Sadie covered his hand with hers. "Carter, maybe I should go in alone," she suggested. "If that kid at the service station recognized you, someone in the store might, too."

Carter's mouth curled downward into a grimace. "You're probably right." He shoved a handful of bills toward her, but she pushed his hand back in his lap.

"I'll use my credit card. Save your cash for now."

Anger darkened his eyes. "I don't want you paying my way."

Sadie rolled her eyes. "Don't be so macho, cowboy. At the moment, the cops have no idea I'm with you so they're not watching my credit card. Later on, if they figure it out, we may have to use your cash."

She let the statement stand between them for a tense second as she watched Carter struggle to accept the truth. He hated relying on her or anyone else, that was obvious.

Because he was a prideful man.

Her heart squeezed, admiration stirring along with regret. Prison must have taken a drastic toll on that stubborn pride, resurrecting her guilt.

She had to help him to ease her conscience.

Besides, she was starting to remember how wonderful it had felt to be in his arms. How potently sexy the man was in bed, and how she'd dreamed of having more than one night with him.

And even though he'd cloaked himself in a coat of armor, beneath that veneer he was a decent man.

He didn't deserve for people to think he was a killer when he'd been framed.

She wanted to see his name cleared, and she was going to help him.

The realization made her feel stronger than she had in years. She and Carter would find out the truth and make Lester pay.

Then they would be free. Finally.

Free to live their lives as they'd dreamed all along.

Maybe even to be together…

She stifled the thought, knowing she had to protect herself from losing her heart to the sexy cowboy. Carter had enough on his plate simply clearing his name. And then he'd need to rebuild his life, not an easy feat after losing five years.

She removed a small notepad and pen from her

purse. "Is there anything specific you want me to pick up?"

A black sedan coasted by them, and Carter settled his Stetson back on his head and slid lower in the seat. "Buy some hair dye and scissors. You can give me a trim. And I need shaving stuff and maybe a ball cap."

They spent the next few minutes making a list. Then Sadie clutched her purse over her shoulder and reached for the car door.

Carter stopped her by placing a hand over hers. "Do you have your gun?"

A tremor rippled through Sadie. "Yes." But it was still daylight and surely Lester hadn't picked up their scent.

She angled her face toward him and pasted on a brave smile. "Don't worry, Carter. I'll be fine."

Carter's eyes darkened. "Just be careful."

Their eyes locked for a moment, a thread of something sensual and sweet rippling between them. Maybe he was starting to care for her after all.

Then again, he had his own agenda. And it didn't involve a romantic entanglement with her.

If Lester killed her, she couldn't give him the alibi he needed to overturn his conviction.

CARTER WATCHED SADIE slip into the store with a sense of unease. What if Lester was working with someone else and they had followed them?

He'd been careful, watching over his shoulder, and hadn't spotted a tail, but he could have easily missed something. Nerves knotted his neck as he scanned the people entering and leaving the store for anyone suspicious. At first glance, he didn't spot anyone who looked out of place. But he kept his eyes trained just in case.

A beefy Hispanic man wearing all black with sleeves of tattoos strolled past the truck, glanced at him with beady eyes, then headed toward the store. Carter sat up straighter, scrutinizing the guy for signs of trouble. His hand itched, and he reached for his gun in case the man recognized him. Two seconds. Three. Four.

Two teenagers in a sedan pulled up and climbed out, music blaring. A heavyset lady parked beside them, worrying with her grandkids as they piled out, begging for candy.

The tattooed man turned around and headed back his way.

Carter clenched his jaw. He had fought in dozens of bar brawls and had engaged in knife fights in prison, all in self-defense. But he'd never shot an innocent man before. If he unloaded on this guy, the cops would come running.

Of course if he worked for Lester, he wasn't exactly innocent.

Palms sweating, he wrapped his fingers around

the pistol's handle, deciding if the man confronted him, he'd hit him with the butt of the gun instead of firing, but suddenly a woman raced up and threw herself at the beefy man. He swung her into his arms and hugged her, then they turned and walked hand in hand back toward the store.

Carter's breath squeezed out of his lungs in a painful rush. The urge to find Sadie and tell her to hurry slammed into him. He didn't like her being out of his sight. Not even for a minute.

But she was right. It was dangerous for him to go inside.

Glancing at the clock, though, he counted the minutes she'd been gone as he crouched lower into the seat. The hundred-degree temperature felt stifling, and sweat dripped down the back of his neck, but he resisted starting the engine and air conditioner.

He had to save his cash. He might need it to pay for some answers.

Seconds later, his cell phone trilled, and he checked the number. Johnny.

He drummed his fingers on the dash as he connected the call. "Johnny?"

"Yeah. How're you doing, man?"

"Sweating like crazy," Carter said. "Have you heard anything from that P.I.?"

"Yeah. He said the last address he found for

Loretta Swinson was Laredo. She's a housekeeper at a local motel." Carter scribbled the name of the motel down as well as the address.

"Thanks, Johnny. Maybe she can point us to Lester or explain why he set me up."

"Good luck." Johnny paused, his breathing rattling over the line. "Listen, Carter, you said you found the Native American woman you saw the night of the murder. Where is she now?"

Carter glanced across the parking lot again, searching for her. She'd been gone a long time now. At least every second felt like an eternity. "We're at a discount store. She's inside buying us some disguises."

A heartbeat of silence passed, tense and fraught with questions. Carter sensed Johnny's disapproval.

"You sure it's smart to keep her with you?" Johnny asked. "The police could add kidnapping charges to your record."

"They don't know she's with me now," Carter says. "And Lester tried to kill her, Johnny. We're safer together."

"I don't know, man—"

"He carved her up with a knife, Johnny, and he's been stalking her ever since." The image of the scar haunted Carter. "I can't let anything else happen to her. I have to find Lester and make him confess the truth or she'll never be safe."

"I thought you hated her," Johnny said quietly.

Carter scrubbed a hand over his face. "I did. But…it's complicated. He…used us both. He threatened her and made her drug me that night."

Another awkward silence. "Just be careful, Carter. She fooled you once before, don't let her do it again."

Carter's gaze shot to the store exit. Johnny's warning reminded him of what had happened years ago. Of waking up disoriented, with blood on his hands, a knife in his hand and the police after him. Of five years of flashbacks where images of Sadie's seduction and betrayal tormented him.

Was she playing him again now? Had she pretended to go along with him, to help him, until she could escape?

No…he didn't think so. That scar…it was real. And she was terrified of Lester.

But he wouldn't let down his guard.

"All the more reason for me to stay with her so I can keep an eye on her," Carter said. Except that she was in the store alone now.

And she *had* fooled him before.

What if she had insisted on going in alone so

she could call the police and turn him in? They might be on their way now....

SADIE'S HANDS TREMBLED as she tossed a prepaid cell phone into the shopping cart. She didn't know if they needed it, but if the police discovered she was with Carter or that his friend had given him a phone, they could run a trace.

She hadn't survived the last five years on the run without learning a few tricks of the trade.

She gathered shaving supplies, scissors, toiletries, hair dye, three different ball caps, a couple of peasant skirts and blouses so she'd have a change of clothes, some T-shirts with sports logos on the front for Carter along with a denim shirt and tie, two scarves, a sunhat for her and a pair of nonprescription glasses and sunglasses for both of them. For a second, she considered a hoodie, but with the temperature soaring she decided that would only draw suspicion.

A noisy cart clanked behind her, and she glanced back to make sure no one was following her. Just a family with two kids. The mother was doling out suckers to entertain the children while the little girl cradled her doll to her chest, and the boy pulled at his sister's pigtails.

A normal family having a normal day.

A pang of sadness engulfed her. At one time

she'd dreamed about a medical career, marriage, a family…

Would her life ever be normal again?

Two Hispanic men walked toward her, and she ducked into the aisle for ladies' underwear, rummaging through the silky panties while she kept one eye on them. They gave her a once-over, then a lecherous grin, and she snatched a package of underwear, tossed it into her cart, and swung down the next aisle, avoiding them.

Thankfully they moved on, but suddenly someone grabbed her arm and jerked her between the fitting room and restroom.

Sadie started to scream, but the man pressed her against the wall with her back to him.

She froze as something hard dug into her back.

Chapter Eight

Sadie's lungs churned for air. "Please don't hurt me—"

A husky sigh breathed against her neck. "I'm not going to, Sadie."

Anger flared inside Sadie and she spun around. "Carter, what are you doing? You scared me to death."

A muscle ticked in his jaw. "I was worried. You've been in here a long time."

"Not that long." Sadie narrowed her eyes, then gestured toward the cart. "Besides, we needed several items," she said. "And you and I discussed this. It's dangerous for you to be in here."

Regret tinged his expression, and he glanced around the store as if to ascertain if they had an audience. A red-haired woman wearing the store smock stood watching, obviously curious. Sadie gave her a quick smile to assure her everything was okay.

When she glanced back at Carter, she sensed

something else was wrong. Then the truth dawned on her. "You thought I might be planning to abandon you, didn't you?" Disappointment and hurt filled her. "Or that I was calling the police to turn you in?"

Guilt slashed across his chiseled face, confirming her suspicions.

"You don't trust me," Sadie said quietly.

Carter shifted sideways leaning against the wall, his face in the shadows. "I...I'm sorry," Carter said. "It's just...I thought—"

"You thought I'd betrayed you before, that I would do it again." In spite of the fact that she understood his caution, her anger rose, and she yanked her arm away. "I realize I left you in the wind before, Carter, but I haven't called anyone. I told you we were in this together and I meant it." She grabbed the cart and pushed it into the aisle. "Now I'm going to pay for this stuff so we can leave."

Carter tucked his hat lower on his head and walked along beside her. "I...want to trust you, Sadie," he said gruffly. "But it's been a long time since I could trust anyone."

Compassion budded inside her. Given his situation, she didn't blame him.

But doubts assailed her. Had he been hardened to the point where he'd never be able to trust her?

Troubled by the thought, she steered the cart through the aisles, staying alert for anyone watching. Carter pressed his hand on the curve of her back as they walked, leaning close to indicate they were a couple.

The idea that they weren't and would never be pained her, but she swallowed her disappointment. She wasn't ready for a relationship anyway.

She had her own nightmares to overcome.

Two of the checkout lines were packed, so she found the self-service lane and began to scan the items. A middle-aged woman with an irritable older woman seemed to be staring at them, and Carter stepped up and nudged her aside. "I got it, sweetheart."

Sadie bit her lip to keep from commenting and planted a big kiss on his cheek. "Thank you, honey. You're so sweet."

"Yeah, real sweet," he said with a sarcastic laugh. Then he dipped his head and laid a liplock on her that curled her toes.

Sadie smiled as he released her, flushed and wanting more. Two teenagers nearby giggled but the older lady shot her a stern look of disapproval.

Carter was still scanning the lines and front of the store, and disappointment ballooned inside her. She wished the kiss had been for real, not an act.

A security guard entered the store, and Carter instantly tensed, then lowered his head and continued scanning the items. Sadie moved up beside him to block the guard's view and bagged their purchases, then swiped her debit card. When the machine asked if she wanted cash back, she punched Yes and withdrew two hundred dollars, which was the maximum it allowed.

She considered asking Carter to stop at another ATM, but the lethal look he shot her silenced her request. His pride was obviously smarting again.

As they strolled to the exit, he threw his arm around her shoulder and she snuggled up to him, kissing his neck. The last thing the police would be looking for was Carter as part of a romantic couple.

"I'll pay you back," Carter said, as they stepped outside and headed to the truck.

Sadie shrugged and opened the truck door. "Don't worry about it." Although worry gnawed at her. Her bank account was lean and without her job, it would quickly dwindle.

Carter clenched his jaw and they finished loading the purchases in the back of the cab in silence. When they climbed in the truck, he covered her hand with his. "I do worry, Sadie. In spite of what you think of me, I'm not a man who uses a woman or takes advantage of her."

Sadie's stomach fluttered. "I know that, Carter. Like I said earlier, all that matters is that we find Lester and clear you so we'll both be free."

Because without that, they would be running forever.

THE MEMORY OF SADIE kissing his neck in the parking lot taunted Carter as he drove toward the motel address where Loretta Swinson worked. He needed to focus on tracking down her and Lester, but he couldn't help but wish the act he and Sadie had put on for the store patrons and employees had been for real.

Because her subtle kisses reminded him of the night they'd made love.

It had been a long time since he'd been close to a woman, and having the one he'd fantasized about while he was locked in a cage so close, and kissing her to boot, was wreaking havoc on his nerves and his deprived libido.

"I talked to Johnny," he said in an effort to distract himself. "His P.I. found an address for Loretta Swinson and her place of employment. She cleans rooms at this motel." He swerved into the motel parking lot, sizing up the place. The pink neon sign and truckers parked in the lot told him it was low rent. A half-dozen bikers in leather screeched up in a circle to the hamburger joint across from the motel.

Carter grimaced. He hated to make Sadie stay in this dive, but they had no choice. But Sadie seemed nonplussed at the run-down conditions, and once again the realization that she'd been running alone, staying in dives like this since he'd been sent away, hit him.

Her predicament was partly his fault. Dammit, he'd like to take her someplace fancy, to a nice restaurant for dinner, to a hotel with satin sheets.

She deserved better than this.

And better than what he could give her even if he was free. He had *nothing,* not a dime to his name. Not a home or any chance of buying one soon.

Sadie reached for the door handle. "You want me to reserve a room or ask for Loretta?"

"The cleaning staff won't show up till morning, so just rent a room. If we ask questions tonight, someone might warn her and she might not show tomorrow."

"Good point." Sadie reached up and touched a strand of his hair. "Then tonight we'll trim and dye your hair."

His body hardened at her simple touch, his mind racing to more intimate things they could do in that room.

Oblivious, Sadie climbed out and walked toward

the entrance to the motel, her long black braid swaying like a rope of silk down her back.

The sound of a motorcycle revving up made him jerk his head around. One of the bikers sped toward the motel entrance, then two kicked into gear and followed.

His window was cracked enough for him to hear, and one of them made a crack about the hot Indian girl who'd just gone inside.

His hand automatically slid to his gun, protective instincts toward Sadie kicking in.

But he couldn't allow his emotions to rule him. As long as they left Sadie alone, he'd stay still.

He needed to find Loretta Swinson and make her talk, not jump into a brawl or get his butt kicked by a bunch of bikers with crude mouths.

One of the other bikers made a joke, then the leader gestured toward the road, and suddenly the gang hit the highway, speeding away.

Relieved, Carter wiped sweat from his face, then scanned the motel lot again. A pickup truck rolled up and two drunken cowboys climbed out, stumbling toward the front with a couple of tramps hugging their sides. Another young couple who couldn't be more than twenty were making out, giggling and kissing as they opened the door to another unit.

Across from the motel, neon signs indicated an

all-night bar with adult entertainment. The urge to see a naked woman and watch her gyrate while he stuffed dollar bills into her G-string was tempting. He'd dreamed about having a woman for so long.

Trouble was, Sadie was the one he wanted to see naked.

And that was not about to happen.

Hell, he had it bad for her. When they finished with Lester and he was free, and Sadie moved on with her life, he'd treat himself to a mindless night of sex.

But not until Sadie was safe.

Besides, the image of her giving him a private lap dance was far more tempting than a stripper who earned her money taking off her clothes for strangers.

Not that Sadie would take her clothes off for him…

She opened the truck door and slid inside. "Room 312, at the far end."

He quirked a brow. "One room?"

She gave him a sour look. "I figured you'd be afraid I'd run off and call the cops if I rented my own."

His heart hammered, making him regret his earlier panic. "Old habits die hard," he admitted.

"I know." She shrugged and worried the beads

at her neck. "Besides, I didn't really want to stay alone tonight."

Her eyes flickered with fear, then oddly something that looked like hunger and need—or maybe he imagined desire in her eyes because he wanted her to want him.

He sure as hell wanted *her*. Just the thought of the two of them sharing a room had his body aching and tied in knots.

A truck roared in, brakes squealing, and he jerked his attention from Sadie. Then a police car swerved up beside it and a cop climbed out.

"Dammit."

Sadie hissed a breath, her gaze cutting toward the truck. "He's after him, not us. Just act casual. Remember, he's looking for you alone, not a couple."

Reminding himself she was right, Carter tugged his hat low over his head then he pulled out and drove to the end of the motel and parked. The police car remained in the lot, but he ignored it, feigning innocence. He and Sadie grabbed the bags, then walked up to the entrance of their room and slipped inside.

As soon as she closed the door, he moved to the window and peered out the side to watch, waiting until the cop finally left. Seconds ticked by, agonizing in their slowness, as if he was walking a dead man's walk.

How much longer would his luck hold out?

Sadie unloaded the toiletries and indicated the bathroom. "Why don't you shave first, then I'll give you a trim and dye your hair."

Carter scrubbed a hand through the shaggy mane, then headed to the bathroom. He unbuttoned his shirt and threw it on the bed, gritting his teeth at Sadie's soft gasp. Undoubtedly she'd seen the jagged scars and knife marks on his back.

"Like you said, we both have scars," he mumbled. He shaved, then sank into the hard wooden seat without offering an apology. He was what he was.

A scarred man on the run with nothing to offer.

She knew the worst of him, so there was no need to pretend otherwise.

He'd had sex with her once. He'd never expected love.

Not a man like him.

Sadie's gaze met his in the mirror, but she lifted her chin, her deep brown eyes flickering with both compassion and a challenge that indicated she wasn't about to run. "No wonder you don't trust anyone."

A tiny smile tugged at the corner of his mouth. "No wonder you don't, either," he said softly.

Sadie surprised him by smiling in return. Sexual tension vibrated between them, then she grabbed a towel, spread it around his shoulders, wet his hair and began to snip the ends.

Carter had never thought having his hair cut was erotic, but watching Sadie lift the strands and run her fingers through the layers sent fire through his blood. The pure intimacy of the act made him shift in the chair to keep from hauling her into his lap.

When she'd evened out the layers, she opened the hair dye, donned the rubber gloves inside the kit, squirted the solution into his hair, then threaded her fingers into the layers and massaged his hand, working the strands all the way to his scalp.

He closed his eyes and moaned. He was in heaven. He only wished it could last.

SADIE WAS GRATEFUL for the momentary connection she felt with Carter. But when he closed his eyes and moaned, desire blazed through her, pummeling her with images of touching Carter's naked back with her fingers and lips.

Of stroking those scars, kissing his pain away and offering herself to him.

He leaned his head back to give her more access, his gesture arousing her tenderness and need to love him more, and she massaged his head, his temple, then the sides of his face. Finally she removed the gloves, and ran her fingers along his neck and the top of his shoulder blades, rubbing at the knots and tense muscles, working her hands to give him a deep tissue massage.

"Sadie," Carter said gruffly. "You don't have to do that."

"Shh," she whispered, her nurturing instincts mingling with the arousal humming through her. "Just relax for a moment."

He made a low sound in his throat, then dropped his head forward and groaned again. His gesture of submission touched her deeply and told her she was earning his trust.

A trust she realized she yearned for more than anything now.

She worked her magic, rubbing her hands together to heat them, then pressing her fingers deeper into his sore, knotted tissue and stroking the tension from his back. His skin felt hot to the touch, his muscles hard, his body so masculine that hunger splintered through her.

For a second, she allowed herself to enjoy the foreign sensations, the need, the burning ache she had for a man to touch her the way she was touching him.

She didn't realize she'd lowered her mouth to his neck until a breath hissed between his teeth.

"Sadie..."

The passionate need in the way he murmured her name triggered a long-dormant hunger to burst inside her, and she trailed kisses along his neck, then lower to the jagged scar at his nape.

Suddenly he jerked around and pulled her head toward him, then claimed her mouth with his. Sadie's head spun as he deepened the kiss and probed her lips apart with his tongue. His hands tunneled through her hair, and he yanked her around in front of him and into his lap.

His thick arousal pulsed against her hip, and fire seeped through her body. He growled deep and low as he plunged his tongue into her mouth and tortured her with his loving, triggering a hundred sensations to ripple through her at once.

Then he began to slowly unfasten the top button of her blouse, his breath hitching as it slipped free and the fabric parted. Panic streaked through her, and she pushed at his chest, as desperate to stop him as she had been to have him moments before.

Her lungs fought for air, and she felt like she was choking, so she turned away. The sight of the bed made her heart pound even harder, and she hurried to the door, flung it open and stepped outside, then leaned against the concrete wall, determined to compose herself.

Tears pricked her eyes. She didn't want to be like this. Afraid to let a man touch her.

Especially when she had wanted, even *craved* Carter's touch.

CARTER'S BODY THROBBED with unspent passion. He wanted Sadie with a vengeance.

But she had run from him as if he was some kind of monster. Was it him? Had he frightened her with his scars? Had he been too rough?

His chest ached with regret, and he stood, tossed the towel on the bathroom sink, then strode into the bedroom. If Sadie didn't want him, he'd accept that.

And if he'd scared her, he'd apologize.

But *she* had kissed *him,* dammit.

Worried about her, he walked to the door. When he spotted Sadie plastered against the wall, trembling, her face ashen, tears glittering on her eyelashes, her hand pressed to the scar on her chest, his stomach heaved.

Something was terribly wrong.

"Sadie?"

"I'm sorry," she said in a raspy whisper. "I..."

"You don't have to apologize," he said gruffly. "Just tell me what I did wrong."

A tormented sound tore from her throat. "It's not you," she said, her voice raw. "It's just...I was smothering."

A sense of dread balled in his stomach. "I was too rough, too pushy—"

"No," Sadie said, whirling toward him. "Don't you understand? It wasn't you."

Anger churned through Carter. "Then it's about Lester."

Her face crumpled then she nodded, pain in her eyes. "I…just…remember him being on top of me, holding me down…I was smothering."

Carter clenched his jaw and braced himself. "Did he rape you?"

Sadie shook her head. "No, but he pinned me down and mauled me and I thought…he was going to. But then he…stopped…he…I think he couldn't finish."

Son of a bitch. Carter wanted to pound his fists against the wall and vent his rage against the man, but acting like a maniac would only frighten Sadie more and prove he was the violent jerk the cops had deemed him to be.

So he forced his voice to an even pitch and stroked her arms gently. "Come on back inside, Sadie. It's not safe out here. Someone could be watching."

Her labored breath tore at his heart. She looked so damn vulnerable that he wanted to pull her into his arms and reassure her that he would never let anyone hurt her again. But he simply lowered his hand and touched her fingers, letting her come to him. She took his hand, then stepped inside.

Their gazes locked for a long moment, then she released a soft sigh of need and frustration that made his blood race. But when she glanced at the single bed in the room and clamped her teeth over her bottom lip, he knew he couldn't push her. That she wasn't ready.

She might never be.

"It's okay," he murmured. He traced a finger along her jaw. "I'll sleep on the floor."

A sad look washed over her face, then relief and a small, self-deprecating smile. "Thank you, Carter."

He didn't deserve her thanks. She should hate him for putting her in the middle of this. "I'm going to wash this stuff out of my hair, then let's drive out to Loretta Swinson's tonight. The sooner we find her, the sooner we can end this nightmare."

Then she could be done with him and free to move on without this constant fear in her life.

IMAGES OF CARTER NAKED, his big, strong body pulsing while water sluiced over him teased Sadie as she listened to the shower running. Her body throbbed with the need to join him while her fears held her locked inside her own private terror.

Carter's reaction to her fleeing his arms earlier

surprised her. Just when she'd expected him to be angry at her, he'd shown compassion.

Judging from his rough exterior, his constant scowl and brooding attitude, people thought he was the hardened criminal the law had portrayed him to be. But she had glimpsed beneath the surface years ago when she'd climbed into his bed.

And tonight…tonight his tenderness had made her heart swell with longing.

She wanted to be whole again, to be able to give herself to him.

The water kicked off, though, and she turned away from the bathroom, knotting her hands in her lap as he strode out wearing nothing but a towel.

Did he have any idea how sexy he looked with his hair damp, water droplets still clinging to that soft dark mat on his chest?

He grabbed the shopping bag with the jeans and other clothing she'd bought, removed a pair of jeans and a T-shirt, then strode back to the bedroom seemingly oblivious to his effect on her.

Five minutes later, he strode back out, dressed and combing his hair. It was lighter now, a sandy brown instead of the brownish-black, and the layers gave it a slight wave.

He put one of the ball caps on his head, then glanced at her as he retrieved his gun. She missed his cowboy hat, but he still looked sexier than any man she'd ever met. "Ready to go?" he asked.

She nodded and stood, then silently followed him out to the truck. He was cautious as usual, and she kept her eyes peeled for police cars or Lester as Carter drove from the parking lot out of town toward Loretta Swinson's place.

The city lights of Laredo faded in the distance, the country opening up. Laredo was one of the oldest border crossing points along the U.S.-Mexican border, and once again she contemplated the two of them running. In Mexico, they would be safe from the police.

But not Lester. He wouldn't care about jurisdiction or the law.

Shivering, she studied the pastures, sandy, rocky areas and the flatland covered in grass, oak and mesquite. Night shadows plagued the horizon, and she searched for stars, but clouds covered them, lending a dismal feel that added to the loneliness gnawing at her. Carter veered down a side street into an area that resembled project housing with overgrown yards and dilapidated concrete homes that reminded her of the reservation houses.

Beat-up cars and two trucks were parked in three of the driveways. The next two houses looked deserted, Condemned signs in the scraggly, dry front yards. At the end of the street, she spotted an adobe structure that didn't look big enough to hold more than two rooms. The windows were broken out, a tree lay splintered in the yard, a rusty Pinto with a flat tire squatted in the drive.

Carter cut the lights then coasted by the house and parked in the cul-de-sac. Sadie gave him a skeptical look, her nerves prickling as they climbed from the truck. Shoulders squared, he rubbed his hand over his gun, visually searching the perimeter as they approached the house.

A dog barked from the woods nearby, and a stray cat darted across the road. The number attached to the concrete front of the house hung askew, the mail slot overflowing with bills and junk mail.

Carter opened the screen door and knocked on the wooden one behind it.

Seconds ticked by as they waited, then Carter leaned against the door frame, listening. "I don't hear anyone inside."

"Maybe she's not home," Sadie whispered.

He frowned, then knocked again and jiggled the doorknob. To her surprise the door squeaked open.

The hair on the back of Sadie's neck stood on end. She'd once thought she had a connection with the earth and spirits, but somewhere along the way she'd lost it. Now, though, she sensed that something was wrong here. The scent of fear and death mingled with the smell of rotting wood and something else she couldn't quite define.

Garbage? Human waste? Blood?

Carter gave her a wary look, motioned for her to stay behind him, then removed his gun and held it at the ready.

She tiptoed in behind him, both of them peering through the darkness. The stench of mold and sour milk filled the air, other acrid odors mingling as if a cat box hadn't been emptied in years.

The front room held a tattered couch and scarred coffee table, magazines and a knitting basket. They inched toward the kitchen. The dirty dishes and glasses littering the counter surprised her. The woman might work as a housekeeper for the motel, but she obviously didn't clean her own home.

The wind picked up, rattling a tree branch against the hall window as they edged toward the bedroom. The sensation that they were walking into a sickening darkness swirled around Sadie, making the room spin. Another odor washed over her, the scent of death.

She'd smelled it with her grandmother, with

other bodies the shaman had lost, with her own mother in her last dying, pain-filled days.

The air shifted, stirring the curtains. The air conditioner? Or a spirit floating nearby? Lost. Hovering. Needing peace.

Gripping the wall to steady herself, she blinked to clear her vision and the nausea rolling through her. The room was so dark that it took a moment for her eyes to adjust. But when they did, she saw a figure in the bed. A woman. Sheets tangled. Limbs askew.

The source of the smell.

Then the light flickered on, bathing the room, and she gasped, swallowing back bile. Loretta was lying faceup, naked, her eyes wide open, her skin a chalky white, the sheets soaked in blood.

She had been murdered.

Chapter Nine

"Dammit," Carter muttered. Loretta was dead. Another lost lead.

It was almost like the killer knew where they were going and was one step ahead.

He crossed the room and felt Loretta Swinson's wrist. "She hasn't been dead long." He whirled around, scanning the room. "Someone knew we were coming."

"What makes you think that?" Sadie asked. "It could have been random—"

"No, my gut feeling says Lester was here. He slashed her throat to keep her from talking to us."

"But she was his alibi."

"Maybe she changed her mind and decided to talk."

Sadie's face paled. "What do we do now?"

Carter gestured around the room. "Let's look around for some clue. Maybe we'll figure out where he's going now."

Sadie touched the woman's stiff white hand.

"We can't just leave her here like this. We have to call the police."

Carter gripped her by both arms and forced her to look away from the blood-soaked sheets and Loretta's ashen face. "Sadie, I know you're in shock, but we can't do that. For God's sake, the cops would probably hang her murder on me, too."

Her mouth slackened. "I…I have to pray for her first. Pray for her spirit."

Carter gritted his teeth. Sadie's faith obviously meant a lot to her, although for the life of him he couldn't understand how she had any faith left after the ordeal she'd suffered.

"All right, but hurry."

Sadie knelt by the woman's side, stroked her forehead, then clasped her hand between her own, rubbed the beads and murmured a Navajo prayer. Carter watched her, admiring her compassion.

Although every second that passed, he sensed the police closing in. What if Lester had killed Loretta and planted evidence to frame him for her murder?

"Come on, Sadie," he said, gently urging her to stand. "For all we know Lester is watching and called the cops. If they find us here, we'll both go to jail."

The sadness in Sadie's eyes turned to alarm, and she straightened. "What are we looking for?"

"Anything that leads us to Lester, something with an address or phone number on it."

Sadie nodded and searched the dresser drawers while Carter rifled through the desk in the corner of the bedroom. Seconds later, he slammed the last drawer shut. "Dammit, nothing."

"Nothing in these drawers, either."

Carter spotted Loretta's purse on the floor, strode toward it, flipped it over and dumped the contents. Two packs of gum, a pack of cigarettes, some loose change, a compact, her wallet and a small address book.

Knowing he needed to hurry, he searched the wallet and found Loretta's ID, then a couple of dollars inside along with a ticket stub to the rodeo at the BBL, but nothing else.

He waved the ticket stub at Sadie. "Loretta was at the rodeo. She must have been watching you for Lester."

"I thought someone was following me then," Sadie admitted.

Suddenly a siren wailed outside, bursting into the silence.

"Carter," Sadie cried. "Do you think the police are coming here?"

"We're not going to wait around and see." He tucked the address book into his pocket.

"Wait." Sadie paused by the nightstand and

grabbed Loretta's cell phone. "We can check her message log."

"Good idea." If Lester had called her, his number would be in her phone. Then they could track him down.

Sadie crammed the phone into her purse, and they ran out the back door just as the siren grew louder. Bright police lights twirled in the distance, creating a rainbow of blue against the night sky. Carter yanked her into the shrubbery banking the property, and they crept behind the bushes.

The police car screeched to a halt, and two policemen jumped out, weapons drawn. Both cops peered around the property, one speaking into his radio as they darted up the front path to the door. The heavier one stayed two steps behind, turning in a wide arc to scan the street, then seemed to pause as he noticed their truck.

Carter pulled Sadie deeper into their hiding spot, hoping the officer wrote the truck off. But the two homes nearest Loretta's were for rent and judging from the dilapidated porches, trash piled on the side of the road and overgrown lawns, obviously vacant.

"Get ready. We may have to run on foot," Carter said.

But they were miles from the town, and that could prove dangerous and timely. Then again, he could try swiping a car from one of the neighbors, but that would be risky, as well.

Carter watched the first cop enter, then the second one started toward Carter's truck, but cop number one yelled back at him. "Get in here and call this in. We got ourselves a murder."

The heavyset cop heaved a breath, jacked up his pants, then turned and lumbered inside the house.

"Let's make a run for it now." Carter urged Sadie behind him, and they raced through the bushes until they reached his truck. Sweat beaded on his neck as he crouched low and they climbed in through the passenger side.

"Stay down," he whispered as he started the engine. He left the lights off, then slid low in the seat, backed the truck up and rolled down the street. But just as he passed Loretta's house, he glanced in the rearview mirror and saw the front porch light flick on and one of the uniforms step outside searching the perimeter.

Carter grimaced. Had the cop taken Carter's license plate? If so, the police would be all over them in no time.

SADIE'S SKIN CRAWLED with nerves as they sped away from the crime scene. The image of that poor dead woman haunted her, the fact that she had once wanted to be a doctor compounding her guilt.

You couldn't have saved her.

The truck bounced over a rut, jarring her and reminding her to fasten her seat belt.

The sound of a police siren wailing rent the night, and she glanced back to see a squad car racing toward them from the opposite direction. Probably backup for the cops at Loretta's house.

The car zoomed by in a blur, and she breathed out in relief. But a minute later, Carter cursed. "Dammit, he made us."

Sadie gripped the door handle and glanced back, her heart pounding as the squad car made a U-turn to chase them.

Carter punched the gas and accelerated, the tires grinding gravel as the truck shot forward. She clung to the door, her heart hammering as Carter swerved down a side dirt road.

"Where are you going?"

"It's a shortcut. Maybe we'll throw them off."

But they had no such luck. The police car swerved and sped up, eating the distance between them. Sadie's pulse jackknifed. They were going to get caught and Carter would go to jail, and she would have to beg for someone to believe her.

Thankfully traffic was minimal, and for the next few minutes Carter wound around the curves, taking several shortcuts to lose the cop.

But he stayed on their tail, closing in. Then out

of nowhere two motorcycles raced toward them, flying as if they were on a racetrack. One tried to pass the other, and Carter swerved to avoid it, screeching along the shoulder of the road.

The cop nearly crashed into the oncoming motorcycle and had to veer right to avoid a head-on collision. He must have overcompensated or lost control, because tires squealed, then he crashed into a boulder, siren still wailing.

Carter drove on, but Sadie was sweating, her hands clenched in her lap. “Do you think he’s hurt?”

“I don’t know.” A vein throbbed in Carter’s neck. “Can you see anything?”

She craned her neck. The motorcycle racers had left him in the wind, dust spewing from their tires, but she spotted the driver’s door open.

“He’s getting out, he’s alive,” she said on a ragged whisper.

The strain on Carter’s face lifted slightly. “Probably calling us in, though, so be on the lookout for more police.”

Sadie sighed wearily. “We need to switch cars. The cops will be looking for this truck.”

Carter’s jaw tightened, then he gave a brief nod. The silence thickened between them as they followed the deserted road, but once they turned onto the main highway leading into Laredo and back toward their motel, another cop climbed on their tail.

Carter made several switchback turns in the city, steering around other cars, through alleys, then ducked into a parking garage and finally lost their tail.

By the time they reached the motel, Sadie's heart was beating so fast she felt like her chest would explode.

Carter pulled the truck around to the back of the parking lot out of sight from the street, and they ducked inside the motel room.

Sadie sank onto the bed, trembling and trying to control her emotions, but the past hour rolled back like a horror show. The chase, the cop crashing his car…the shock of seeing Loretta brutally murdered…

That could have been her, her throat slashed…

Carter paced the room, his agitation adding to her nerves. "Dammit, we're not any closer to the truth now than we were before. And now Loretta's dead we've lost that lead."

"But if Lester killed her, that confirms your suspicions."

"It doesn't matter," Carter said, his jaw clenched. "The police are looking for me. They'll think I killed her just like they think I killed Dyer."

"Then we'll prove you didn't do it." Sadie remembered the woman's cell phone in her purse and laid it on the table. "Why don't you look at this and see what you can find and I'll go get us something to eat."

"I'm not hungry," Carter said.

Sadie rubbed her arm. She needed some air, to think for a minute. The room, the shock of seeing Loretta murdered…it triggered all the memories of her attack. Of Lester's hands on her.

Nausea climbed to her throat. She wanted to help Carter, but she had to escape him at the same time. At least for a few minutes. "We'll figure it out together, Carter." Sadie bundled her hair into a scarf. "I'm going to walk to the burger joint across from the motel and pick us up some dinner. I'll be right back."

Carter caught her hand before she left. "Sadie, I don't want you out there alone."

Sadie's gaze met his, her stomach fluttering with nerves. She didn't like it either, but they had no choice. And she didn't want to lose control in front of Carter. He needed her to be strong now, not to fall apart. "I'll be fine. Remember they're looking for you, not me."

Carter shook his head. "But Lester wants *you*."

Sadie squeezed his hand and patted her purse where she kept the gun. "Don't worry. I'll be right back, then we'll decide what to do."

Carter hesitated another moment, but finally took Loretta's phone and released her. Sadie stepped outside and collapsed against the concrete wall for a moment, her breathing choppy. A panic attack threatened and her stomach roiled, the heat cloying.

Desperate to regain her composure, she stroked the beads around her neck, then closed her eyes, relying on the image of her mother to calm her, on the sound of her voice murmuring prayers in the Navajo language. Of the spiritual lessons she'd learned and the inner peace she craved, a balance between fear and courage. She heard the natives of the tribal community chant, saw the sandpainting healing ceremony in her mind and felt her faith returning.

Seconds later, she opened her eyes, feeling calmer, her stomach less queasy. She scanned the parking lot as she crossed it, one hand inside her purse in case she needed the gun. Still, by the time she entered the fast-food restaurant, she was perspiring and had a knot in her throat.

A couple of teenagers, an elderly lady and a man were seated eating, a Hispanic man with a lizard tattoo on his neck standing in line. A biker jerked past her, his leather jacket brushing her arm as he passed.

She stepped in line, then the bell on the door

tinkled behind her, and she glanced up at the security mirror attached to the wall and saw two men who looked like plainclothes cops, maybe federal agents, enter, their gazes sweeping the room as if looking for someone.

Sadie forced herself to act naturally as she placed her order, but she felt the men's gazes burn her back and wondered if somehow they'd figured out that she was helping Carter.

Or that she had been inside the dead woman's house earlier.

CARTER PUSHED ASIDE the curtain and watched the parking lot to make sure Sadie made it safely to the restaurant. The moment she'd gone in, though, he'd had a sense of loss.

What if something happened to her while she was inside? What if he couldn't save her?

Panic threatened to choke him, but he reined in his fear, reminding himself that he had to control himself.

But he would not allow Lester to hurt Sadie.

Which meant he had to locate the man before he found them.

Since his escape, he'd been living on borrowed time. With Loretta's murder, that time was about to run out.

His pulse pounding, he flipped on the TV

set while he retrieved the woman's phone and scanned the phone log history.

Several calls to the motel and some take-out restaurants showed up, then a local number popped up repeatedly. He checked the messages and found two that Loretta hadn't deleted. The first one was a dead end, from a drugstore saying her prescription was ready. The second one was from a girlfriend warning her that she'd spotted Lester. The woman sounded nervous, even scared.

Carter punched Redial, his anxiety mounting as he waited on the phone to ring. Moments later, a woman answered.

"Hello."

"Listen, you don't know me, ma'am, but you obviously knew Loretta Swinson."

A deep man's voice rumbled in the background. "I told you not to answer my phone, Mama."

Carter tightened his fingers around the hand-set. That voice…he recognized it from the night of Dyer's murder.

It was Lester.

"Who is this?" the woman asked in a shaky voice.

Carter's first instinct was to demand to speak to Lester, to request a meeting.

But he had to think smart. Lester might have other men working with him. Suddenly the man's voice echoed over the line. "Who the hell is this? And what are you doing with Loretta's phone?"

Carter disconnected the call, his mind racing. Maybe he could get Johnny's P.I. to trace the number.

Better yet, he'd talk to Sadie. They would set a trap for Lester.

He glanced at the clock, his nerves on edge as he stood and paced back to the window. Sadie exited the burger joint, tugging the scarf around her hair and clutching the food with one hand. Two men in suits stepped from the fast-food place behind her, making Carter's panic rise.

They looked like feds.

Dammit.

Sadie crossed the street, cars blaring, then rushed to the room. He threw open the door and ushered her inside just as a special news flash aired on the television set in the corner.

"Laredo police have just reported that they are investigating the homicide of a woman named Loretta Swinson. Ms. Swinson was found murdered tonight at her home. A man and woman were seen leaving the crime scene and are considered persons of interest."

The reporter flashed Carter's mug shot on air. "Carter Flagstone, an escaped prisoner convicted of murder, is thought to be the man in question.

Police consider him armed and dangerous and at this point, are uncertain if the woman is a hostage or an accomplice, but warn residents and anyone who may come in contact with them to please be careful. If you spot Flagstone, do not approach him. Call the police immediately."

Sadie staggered against the wall. "This is not good. Now they know there's two of us."

Carter grabbed the bags of clothing and toiletries. "There were two men following you outside the burger joint. We need to get out of here."

"I thought they might be undercover cops," Sadie said.

"They probably traced Loretta's work address here. Come on."

Sadie clutched the food bags and followed Carter to the door. He eased it open and spotted the two men climbing into a dark sedan across from the motel. They'd probably already checked with the registration desk for couples staying at the motel and were staking them out.

Carter motioned for Sadie to wait at the door, and he stood on edge until an eighteen-wheeler pulled into the parking lot, blocking the cops' view. Then he ducked low and coaxed her to follow him around the back of the motel.

They ran for a mile until they reached another seedy motel, and Carter spotted a beat-up station wagon parked at one end that was unlocked, one window broken.

"Get in," he told Sadie. "And stay low."

She jumped in the passenger side, and he climbed in the driver's seat and hot-wired the vehicle. Sadie's eyes widened when she realized what he was doing, but she refrained from commenting. Instead, she fastened her seat belt and held on tight as he cruised away from the motel and into town.

"What do we do now?" Sadie asked.

"Go to another motel. This time use a fake name."

"Did you find anything from Loretta's phone log?"

"Yes, and I have an idea." He pushed Loretta's phone into her hands. "I want you to call the number. It's Lester's phone."

Sadie gasped. "What? I…can't."

Carter covered her hand with his. "Yes, you can, Sadie. This has to end. And the only way we can do that is to set a trap for Lester."

Chapter Ten

Sadie twisted her hands in her skirt. Did Carter have any idea the depth of what he was asking her to do? How painful it would be for her to talk to Jeff Lester, to hear his voice again?

A voice that had haunted her day and night for five long years.

A voice she'd prayed she'd never hear again.

"Sadie?" Carter stroked the base of her neck with his thumb. "I know it won't be easy, but we have to catch this guy before he kills us."

Somewhere in her subconscious Sadie knew Carter was right, but the memory of Lester carving that X in her chest was so vivid and strong that she felt momentarily paralyzed. She could feel his breath on her face, his hands around her neck, the knife digging into her skin....

Carter swung the car down a side street, then into an alley until he found another road leading out of the city. The smell of greasy burgers and fries suddenly turned her stomach, and silence stretched between them, ticking with tension as he headed north.

Finally Carter stopped at a motel in the middle of nowhere. Only one other car was in the lot, the place shrouded by trees.

"Go in and rent us another room. We'll eat and then make the call."

Sadie's nerves pinged. But the scar on Carter's face, the one that hadn't been there before prison, reminded her what Lester had done to both of them. So she nodded, moving on autopilot as she opened the car door.

In spite of the suffocating heat, a chill engulfed her as she walked up to the motel entrance and stepped into the ramshackle lobby. But she forced a smile at the young twenty-something wannabe cowboy. The scrawny kid could never measure up to Carter.

"How many rooms?" the boy asked.

"Just one," she said, then handed him enough cash for the night.

She signed the register using a fake name, then rushed back to the car.

Carter parked around back again, and they slipped inside. The motel room was dingy, the pea-green carpet musty, the bedding a faded green and beige that reeked of beer, sex and dirty bodies.

Carter closed the door, pitching them in darkness, then drew the shades before he flipped on the bathroom light. Sadie had stayed in roach motels, but this one was the pits.

Carter wolfed down a burger. Sadie tried to eat, but she could only manage a couple of bites before she pushed away the food. Images of Lester attacking her flashed through her mind, but she pictured him slashing Loretta Swinson's throat, and her resolve kicked in.

Loretta had helped Lester kill Dyer and frame Carter.

Had he threatened Loretta and forced her into covering for him?

Or had the poor woman loved the jerk and been seduced into helping him?

Either way, it was obvious Lester hadn't loved her.

To Lester, a person's life meant nothing.

He couldn't get away with murder.

Not anymore.

"Okay, Carter." Pasting on a brave face, she sipped her soda. "What should I say to Lester when I talk to him?"

Carter's eyes darkened with concern, and he moved to sit beside her. "Tell him you know where I am. That you'll make a deal with him."

Sadie frowned, confused. "What kind of deal?
"That you'll set a trap for me if he'll leave you alone."

SADIE SHOOK HER HEAD. "No, Carter, I won't give you up."

Carter's rage mounted at the tremor in Sadie's tone.

Forget what the creep had done to *him*.

He wanted revenge for Sadie.

And that poor Swinson broad.

He'd used her and thrown her away like a piece of trash. No woman deserved that.

He captured her hands in his. "Listen to me. Lester is going to find us one way or the other, and I want to confront him on my terms. This way I'll have the advantage."

Her eyes softened, tearing at his heart. "But I don't want him to hurt you. Maybe we should go to the police."

"You know good and well they'll shoot me before they'll listen. And then Lester will escape."

Sadie curled her hands into his.

"If you can't do it, Sadie, I'll call—"

"No." Sadie straightened her spine, determination lighting a fire in her eyes. "You're right. It's time for us to expose Lester so everyone will know the truth."

He offered her an encouraging smile and released his grip on her, then handed her Loretta's phone. Her hand looked surprisingly steady as she punched Redial. Carter's heart throbbed painfully in his chest as he leaned close to hear the conversation.

"All right, Flagstone," Lester growled. "I know it's you."

Sadie stroked the prayer beads at her neck. "No, it's me, Sadie Whitefeather."

A surprised grunt echoed over the line. "Well, well, well, my little *chiquita.* You miss your old friend?"

Carter gritted his teeth at the look of anger that flashed across Sadie's face. But better anger than cold fear.

"Listen to me, Lester. I'm tired of you watching me. I'll make you a deal."

Lester muttered a sarcastic sound. "You're getting brave, darlin'."

"I just want you off my back," Sadie said with more conviction.

A tense silence vibrated for a millisecond, then Lester grunted. "What are you offering?"

"I know where Carter Flagstone is."

"You'll give him up?" Lester coughed. "Hell, I thought you were screwing the cowboy."

"Not since he escaped," Sadie said. "He hates me now."

"You ain't that woman the cops seen him with?"

Sadie lowered her voice to a whisper. "Yes, I am. But he's been holding me at gunpoint. I finally snuck this phone away from him, and I'm hiding in the bathroom."

"How do I know this isn't a setup?"

"Just think about it, smart guy. You know I was the reason Carter went to jail. You really think he and I are friends now?"

Her gaze met Carter's, and his throat swelled with emotions. He *had* hated her for so long that he'd thought he'd wring her neck when he finally found her.

Now he'd give his life—and his freedom—to protect her.

He just hoped they both didn't die trying to settle this score.

"All right. Where do I find him?" Lester asked.

Sadie licked her lips, and Carter mouthed directions.

"He's heading over to the liquor store near our motel." Sadie gave him the address. "And remember, once you take care of him, we're done. No more stalking me. No more threats."

"How do I know you won't go to the police and tell them I killed Flagstone?" Lester shot back.

"If I planned to go to the cops, I would have called them instead of you." Sadie looked up at

Carter, her eyes swimming with turmoil. "I want him and you out of my life for good."

Lester hesitated, his breathing heavy over the line. "All right," he finally agreed. "But if you do call the cops, I'll find you again." His voice dropped a decibel. "And next time that knife will go clean through your heart."

Anger and fury spiked Carter's adrenaline at the man's vile words. Sadie paled, then gave him a bleak nod as she disconnected the call. "Carter—"

He pulled her up against him and wrapped his arms around her. "It's going to be okay, Sadie. I promise I won't let him hurt you."

She leaned into his embrace. "Just be careful. I…don't want anything to happen to you."

Carter's lungs tightened at the way she fit into his arms. It was the first time in years someone actually sounded like they gave a damn about him.

And she was the first person he'd cared about, as well.

Finding Lester was the only way to make them both whole again.

He wouldn't let her down.

FEAR CLAWED AT SADIE as Carter yanked on the denim jacket she'd bought, then checked his gun and headed to the door. What if their plan went awry and Carter was injured? Or worse, killed?

Itching to do something herself, she crossed the room to him. "Carter, wait. I don't want you to go out there alone."

Carter tilted his head sideways, his eyes darkening. "Don't tell me you're worried about me, Sadie."

Her heart fluttered. She hated to show her weakness for the man, that she was falling for him, but she couldn't lie, either. "What if I am?"

A slow smile softened the harsh planes of his face. Then he lifted his hand and feathered her bangs away from her forehead with his fingers. "I've tangled with worse than Lester in prison and survived."

"But he has a gun," Sadie whispered. "And for all we know he may be working with a partner."

Carter shrugged off her concern. "I survived prison. I'll survive this."

Sadie frowned. "Your life is not something to take lightly," she said. "All life is sacred."

Carter arched a brow. "So you only care because of your Navajo beliefs?"

A blush heated Sadie's cheeks. "No."

Carter's breath whispered out, then he pressed his lips against hers. Sadie sighed and leaned into him, then stroked his cheek, savoring the kiss. His tongue probed her lips apart and she welcomed him inside, aching for more and suddenly terrified that this might be the last chance she had to be close to him.

She wanted more.

But Carter pulled away, then brushed her cheek with the palm of his hand. "If anything happens to me, Sadie, promise me you'll call Johnny Long. He'll protect you and make sure that Lester gets caught."

Sadie's throat clogged with tears. "Carter—"

"Shh." He pressed his finger to her lips then removed the car keys from his pocket. "Now, take the keys to the car and drive down the street and wait. Lester doesn't know what kind of vehicle we're driving, but he knows this motel is near the liquor store. He might come here first."

Sadie's legs felt quivery, but she nodded and took the keys.

"If you see him, Sadie, don't wait on me. Drive away, call Johnny and ask him to meet you at the BBL. I'll meet up with you after I find out why Lester set me up."

Sadie searched his face. Was he trying to get rid of her because he planned to kill Lester?

She bit her tongue to keep from asking as he opened the door and tugged her toward the station wagon. Then she climbed inside, started the engine and drove from the parking lot down the street as Carter had instructed.

But she positioned herself near the alley where she could watch when Carter passed it on foot to the liquor store. Her hand trembled as she pulled her derringer from her purse and flicked off the car lights.

Every life was sacred.

She'd been taught that by her people.

But Carter had suffered enough because of Lester.

If he tried to sabotage Carter, she'd defend him.

CARTER SCANNED THE PERIMETER of the motel, the parking lot, the dark side street that led down to an abandoned warehouse row. He didn't see Lester.

But he *felt* him.

Sensed that the bastard was watching as he had been for years. Keeping tabs on him in prison and on Sadie every time she'd moved.

So where was he hiding?

He tried to steady his breathing, remembered the skills he'd honed in prison, how to focus his senses on every sound around him, every smell, every prickly feeling that rippled up his neck.

Relying on those instincts had kept him alive.

It would do so now and help him catch Lester.

He cut his eyes to the left then right, his boots

cracking against the gravel as he strode into the liquor store. Red lighting advertised the beer and wine section, the hard liquors showcased by a bear-crossing sign pointing to the wall.

He'd craved a cold beer in the pen, but tonight his gut yearned for whiskey. He headed toward the bourbon, scanning the bar for Lester.

Maybe he'd have reason to celebrate after he confronted him.

Instead he spotted a kid barely old enough to drive sneaking a bottle of rum in his black leather jacket. The kid spotted him and gave him a threatening glare, and Carter choked back a laugh. The kid had no idea he was a convicted felon who could tear him apart in seconds.

But he reminded him of himself at that age, so he shrugged it off. Let the owner of the store deal with him.

He chose a bottle of bourbon from the shelf, tugging his baseball hat low on his head as he stepped up to the cash register. An elderly lady with sun-tarnished skin and white hair looked up from her gun magazine long enough to ring his purchase and take his cash, but thankfully didn't pay him any attention.

He tucked the brown bag inside his denim jacket, glanced once more around the store and noticed the kid was fidgeting as he approached the register. Then he stepped outside. Another glance in all directions. Nothing.

In fact, except for a Jeep with another kid inside, obviously waiting on his friend, the parking lot was eerily silent.

Carter clenched his teeth. He knew Lester was here though. Skulking somewhere in the shadows. Waiting to pounce.

Taking shallow breaths to slow his heart rate, he crossed the lot heading toward the motel, his senses alert, listening for the tiniest sound. The crack of a twig. The scrape of a shoe. A rock skittering in the dirt.

A breath.

He was inches from the alley when the sound of a gun being cocked reverberated in the silence. He heard the sound of the bullet skimming through the air, then drew his gun and jumped aside just in time for the shot to miss him.

Flattening himself against the concrete wall of the building on the corner of the alley, he swung his weapon out then peered into the shadows. A footstep scuffing the cement made him glance to the left, and he spotted the silhouette of a man.

"Come on out and face me, Lester," Carter said, using the building corner to shield him. "You framed me. The least you can do is tell me the reason."

"Damn you, Flagstone," Lester growled. "You should have died in prison."

"But I didn't," Carter said. "And you picked the wrong man to screw with."

A sinister chuckle rent the air. "I picked a drunk with a bad attitude. You were the perfect patsy."

Carter couldn't argue with that point. "I'm not a dumb kid anymore," he said in a lethal tone.

Another shot pinged toward Carter and he raced into the alley, dodging it. He had to get to Lester. Footsteps clattered. Lester cursed.

Another shot ripped toward him, and he dove to the side to dodge it, but suddenly he spotted another shadow in the alley from the opposite end of the street.

Sadie!

Dear God… "Go back, Sadie!" Carter yelled.

Lester lunged toward her and Carter fired. Lester bellowed a curse, then spun around and fired at Carter.

Carter swerved sideways to avoid the shot, but the bullet pierced his stomach with a fiery burn that rocked him back on his heels. Sadie screamed and started toward him, but Lester raised his weapon and fired at her.

Carter aimed at Lester and pulled the trigger, then pressed his hand to his gut to stem the bleeding. Lester inched toward him, hiding in the shadows, but Carter fired again.

Then Lester's body slumped to the ground.

The pain made Carter weak, and he staggered. But he had to get to Lester, had to make him talk. He couldn't let him escape.

Sucking air through his teeth, he spat out the bile filling his throat, then staggered down the alley toward Lester, keeping his gun trained on the man. Sadie raced toward him.

"Carter, you're hit," she cried.

"I know, but have to make Lester talk."

Fear strained her face, but she slid her arm around his waist to support him, and helped him hobble toward Lester.

Defeat weighed on him as he drew closer to Lester. He wasn't moving.

Dammit, Lester couldn't be dead. Then he'd never talk...

Blinking away the dizziness, he staggered closer. By the time he reached Lester, Carter was sweating and shaking.

"Come on, Carter, let me take you to the hospital," Sadie whispered.

"No, no hospital." He grunted in pain then dropped to his knees beside Lester's body.

Lester's hand shot up and he grabbed Carter's arm, then Lester gasped for air. A faint light from a building in the distance reflected off the pavement, revealing blood soaking Lester's shirt. Carter had hit him in the chest.

Lester coughed up blood, his arm jerking violently, his grip loosening until his hand fell limply to the ground.

Carter grunted and aimed his gun at Lester's head.

"It's time you told me what's going on."

Lester shook his head.

Carter clenched the man's chin with an ironclad grip. "Why did you kill Dyer? Why me?"

"Told you—"

"I know, because I was drunk. But why kill Dyer?"

Lester's eyes slid closed, his body convulsing.

Carter shook him. "Tell me, dammit!"

Lester slowly opened his eyelids, blood dribbling from the side of his mouth. "Ask your old man…"

"What kind of game are you playing? My old man is dead," Carter growled.

"He…knew…"

Lester's words trailed off as a labored breath rasped from his chest, then his body went slack, his eyes staring wide into space.

Dammit. Lester was dead.

Chapter Eleven

Sadie was so terrified she could barely breathe. Lester was dead, and Carter was losing blood so fast that he would die, too, if she didn't get him some help.

"Carter," Sadie whispered. "We have to get you to a hospital."

He didn't seem to hear her, though. He leaned his head on his hand and heaved for air. Sweat was pouring off of him, and his body was shaking. He was going into shock.

"What did Lester mean?" Carter asked, his breathing choppy. "My father knew—"

The sound of a siren burst into the night, its wail jarring Sadie. "Carter, someone must have heard the gunshots and called it in. We have to go."

He looked up at her through a fog of pain and shock. "Help me stand."

She braced her weight to help him, wincing as he stumbled and nearly collapsed on top of

Lester. But he made a sound of determination in his throat then clung to her as she pulled him up and steadied him. Leaning on her, they hurried down the alley toward the station wagon.

By the time they reached it, he was moaning and having a hard time staying on his feet. Worried he was going to pass out before they could escape, she propped him against the car while she opened the door. He collapsed inside the passenger seat just as the lights of the police car shattered the night.

Adrenaline surged through Sadie, and she ran to the driver's side, jumped in, started the car and backed out of the alley. Police lights swirled against the darkness from the motel side, then tires screeched and the police car veered into the alley.

She eased the car to the corner, and forced herself to drive slowly so as not to call attention to them both, crawling through the first red light, then easing through town. When she reached the outskirts, she veered onto the highway heading away from the area.

Carter moaned, his head lolling back. His pallor was gray and ashen, his jaw slack. Blood was seeping from his belly, worrying her more.

She reached behind her and grabbed one of the bags of clothes, removed two T-shirts she'd bought for him, then balled them up and laid them on his belly. "Carter, press these to your wound."

He grunted, but allowed her to lift his hand and place it against his injury, although his eyes were rolling back in his head. When she checked his pulse, it was weak and thready. Realizing he didn't have the energy to exert enough pressure to stem the blood flow, she used one hand to apply pressure herself and steered with the other.

"Carter," Sadie said in a low voice. "I'm scared. If you don't get help, I…don't know what will happen. I…can't lose you now."

"No hospitals. The cops will track me there." Carter's eyes flickered open for a brief second, then his gaze met hers. "You…have training," he rasped. "You can remove the bullet."

For a brief second, terror flitted through her. She'd never operated on anyone before.

But he would die if the bullet wasn't removed.

Touching her beads for comfort, she made a snap decision. She'd take him to the reservation, to the shaman who had tended to her after her attack.

Maybe together they could save his life.

CARTER GRITTED HIS TEETH against the pain, the world around him blurring. In spite of his best efforts to stay alert, he drifted in and out of consciousness. The bitter taste of blood and sweat and the realization that he was dying taunted him.

Dammit, he had survived childhood beatings, then gang assaults in prison. He'd been stabbed by a knife and a screwdriver in jail, had fractured bones and concussions. And he'd nearly lost a foot when his first cellmate had dropped a brick on it and he'd gotten a staph infection.

And when that bus had crashed and he'd escaped, he'd expected the cops to surface and shoot him in the back.

But he had lived through all that.

He refused to die now.

Not until he cleared his name.

The car bounced over a jut in the road, jarring him, and blood seeped through the T-shirts Sadie had pressed onto his wound. Sadie…

He tried to open his eyes and look at her, to memorize her face just in case something happened and he never saw her again. Because if he did die, he wouldn't be going to heaven, and Sadie would.

She looked like a damn goddess, strands of that silky black hair slipping from her braid, her delicate jaw set in determination. He struggled to open his mouth and make his voice work, to thank her, to ask where they were going, but he didn't have the energy.

Reminding himself the police were still after him, he struggled to listen for sirens, but barring the quiet drone of the engine and an occasional car whipping past on the long deserted road, the night was blissfully quiet.

Weak and drained, he closed his eyes and let the steady rumbling of the car on the road lull him into sleep. He'd rest for a few minutes. Save his energy. They were safe now.

At least with Lester dead, *Sadie* was safe.

He wouldn't be until the cops stopped chasing them. And he wouldn't quit investigating until he discovered what Lester had meant about his old man.

But he had to let Sadie go. She would be better off without him. Safer. Free of the police.

Free to move on and have a life, the life she'd wanted before he and Lester had screwed it up. The life she deserved.

Only he couldn't be a part of it.

WORRY KNOTTED SADIE'S STOMACH as she drove toward the reservation. Judging from Carter's ashen pallor, the blood soaking the shirts she'd used as a pressure gauge and his shallow, labored breathing, he was growing weaker by the minute.

What if she couldn't save him?

He had told her to go to his friend for help if he died, but she refused to believe that would happen.

Carter had suffered too much already; she would not lose him.

Her heart squeezed, emotions welling in her throat. They had come too far to give up now.

Nervous tension riddled her body every time she passed a car, and she constantly scanned the area for the police, listening for siren sounds to approach any second.

She flipped on the radio, hoping to find a country station to soothe her anxiety, and was relieved to hear a Crystal Bowersox original. Her rich, honest melody flowed through the speakers, giving Sadie hope that her faith would help her through this ordeal.

Seconds later, a news report interrupted the music, and a sense of trepidation filled her as she listened.

"Police outside Laredo found the body of a man identified as Jeff Lester tonight. He was shot and was pronounced dead at the scene of the fatal shooting." The reporter paused. "Police claim a witness spotted a man and woman leaving the scene. They believe the man was escaped prisoner Carter Flagstone, who was identified from a security camera at the liquor store close to the alley where the murder occurred.

"They have also identified the woman traveling with him as Sadie Whitefeather, an advocate for the Native American community. At this point, police believe Ms. Whitefeather is helping Flagstone and are also looking at her as a person of interest in the homicide."

Perspiration trickled down the front of Sadie's blouse as the reporter trailed off, relaying phone numbers for people to call in case they spotted her and Carter.

"Sadie," Carter mumbled. "You should go to the police, tell them the truth, save yourself…"

"Shh, don't worry about it," Sadie said, as she crossed into the reservation. "We're here now and we're going to tend to that gunshot wound."

Carter mumbled something she didn't understand, then passed out again. Sadie whipped the car down the graveled road leading into the reservation, bypassing several houses and two hogans, and driving straight toward Jimmy Blackhorse's.

She and Jimmy had grown up together, and he'd been a wonderful friend when she'd been assaulted. She pulled to a stop in front of his small adobe house, pummeled by memories of the two of them growing up together as children. Darkness bathed the front yard, yet a light burned low in the front room, and Sadie pictured Jimmy inside, reading, meditating, working on some environmental issue to help improve the farming on the reservation.

She cut the engine, then turned to check on Carter. He was unconscious, a fine sheen of sweat soaking his face and chest. She lifted her hand from the wound and felt the stickiness of his blood on her palm. "Carter," Sadie whispered. "I'm going to get help. I'll be right back."

He moaned slightly as if he'd heard her, and she pressed his hand on top of the blood-soaked cloth. Knowing every minute counted, she jumped from the vehicle, jogged to the door and pounded on it.

A second later, the door swung open and Jimmy stood in the door frame, a surprised look on his face. "Sadie, what are you doing here?"

"I need your help."

Disappointment momentarily flickered across his face. She'd known he wanted more from her when she'd stayed on the reservation, but to her Jimmy would always simply be a friend.

He crossed his arms. "What's going on? I heard on the radio that you were seen with some felon. The police are looking for you."

"I know." Sadie sighed. "Please, Jimmy, you have to trust me." She gestured toward the car. "Carter's hurt, he's been shot—"

"For God's sake, Sadie, you brought a wanted criminal here to the reservation?"

Sadie winced at the condemnation in his voice. "I know, it's dangerous. But he's innocent, Jimmy.

I...please just help me and I'll explain everything."

For a heartbeat, Sadie thought he intended to deny her, but then he pushed past her and strode to the car. "What happened?"

"We were attacked in an alley." Sadie hurried along beside him. "Carter was shot in the stomach, and he's lost a lot of blood."

Jimmy opened the driver's side, then felt for Carter's pulse. When he looked up at Sadie, his expression turned grave. "We need the shaman, and that bullet will have to be removed. I'll get some medical supplies inside, then we'll take him to Spirit Eagle."

He rushed inside and returned moments later with gauze and a medical bag. Sadie drove the car and followed Jimmy in his truck, then they parked at Spirit Eagle's hogan.

Spirit Eagle was aging, over seventy now, with white hair and a beard. His leathery skin was wrinkled and sagging, but he was the wisest man she'd ever known. His calm, spiritual manner always comforted Sadie, and he had taught her the ways of their people.

He also had built a sweatbox in the woods on the hill behind his property and had erected a tent for spiritual ceremonies and prayer.

"I sensed you would be coming," Spirit Eagle

said, as he rested his gray eyes on her. "You are in much need of prayer, my child."

"Yes, but first we have to take care of my friend. He's been wounded and has lost a lot of blood."

Spirit Eagle gestured for her to bring Carter inside, and she and Jimmy returned to the car to retrieve him. Carter moaned, incoherent, as they helped him into the small house.

Spirit Eagle's moccasin-clad feet barely made a sound as he gathered herbs and plants to make a healing compress.

Carter collapsed onto the cot, and Jimmy hurried to heat water and tear some strips of cloth for bandages, while Spirit Eagle examined Carter. "The bullet is deep."

"I know," Sadie said.

"I'm afraid you must take over. My hands are no longer steady enough." Spirit Eagle held out his hands, which had become even more gnarled with arthritis than when she'd seen him last. He also had developed a fine tremor, indicating Parkinson's.

Sadie ached for him, but panic threatened her at the thought of cutting into Carter. What if she made a mistake?

Spirit Eagle laid a gentle hand on Sadie's shoulders. "Breathe in deeply and have faith, my Sadie.

You were born to be a doctor. You have healing hands."

If she had healing hands, why couldn't she have saved her mother?

"Your mother's death was not your fault, my dear one," Spirit Eagle said in that eerie way he had of reading her mind. "It was her time. Such is the cycle of life."

Heat from Spirit Eagle's palm seeped into Sadie's back, comforting her, and she closed her eyes, summoning her faith and courage. If ever she needed to believe in herself, in the lessons Spirit Eagle had taught her and in the emergency medicine she'd picked up volunteering at the hospital, it was now.

Knowing Carter's life depended on her, she opened her eyes and nodded at Spirit Eagle, indicating she was ready. Jimmy brought a pan of steaming water and sterilized a scalpel, scissors, a needle and tweezers.

"Help me remove his jacket," Sadie said.

Jimmy lifted Carter's shoulders and she tugged at the sleeves, the two of them working quickly together to shed the jacket. She spotted the bottle of liquor tucked into the inside pocket at the same time Jimmy did.

Carter groaned and pulled at her arm. "Sadie—"

"I'm right here, Carter," Sadie said, desperate

to soothe him. "I'm going to remove the bullet, then we'll dress the wound."

Jimmy opened the bottle of whiskey. "Here, he should drink. It will help dull the pain."

Sadie lifted Carter's head at an angle and tilted the bourbon to his mouth. "I don't have any anesthetic, Carter. Drink some whiskey before I start."

His eyes opened to slits, the pain glazing them over, and he wheezed a breath but sipped from the bottle. When he'd had a couple of long drinks, she handed the bottle to Jimmy, then took the scissors and began to cut Carter's shirt.

As the bloody fabric fell away, she peered at the wound to determine how deeply the bullet was embedded. If it was a through-and-through, it would have been simpler, but the bullet had lodged a couple of inches in his abdominal wall.

Hopefully it hadn't damaged any major organs, but she couldn't be sure. He needed to be in a hospital, tests run, an experienced doctor, a transfusion, antibiotics…

All the things lacking here on the reservation.

"You okay, Sadie?" Jimmy asked.

Perspiration beaded on her forehead, but she murmured yes, then grabbed the scalpel and eased the point into Carter's belly. His muscles clenched, and he moaned, then ground his teeth in an effort to control the pain. A second later, he passed out.

She peeled back layers of tissue, then finally spotted the bullet. Using the tweezers, she carefully removed it then dropped it into the aluminum pan Jimmy held for her.

Then she wiped her brow with the back of her arm and methodically pressed gauze to his wound to soak up the fresh blood.

Jimmy acted as her assistant, passing her hydrogen peroxide to clean the wound and discarding the bloody gauze, then handing her fresh gauze as needed. When she had the bleeding under control, she stitched up the wound and dressed it.

By the time she was finished, her legs felt shaky, and she was drenched in sweat. Jimmy set a pan of cool water on the bedside table, then left the room, and she used it to wipe Carter's face and neck. He moaned and tried to open his eyes, but he was too weak to do anything but mumble her name.

"The bullet is out now," Sadie whispered.

But the next few hours, maybe days, would tell. He needed fluids and IV antibiotics, but they would have to make do with herbal remedies and what they had here.

Spirit Eagle had slipped outside while she was dressing Carter's wound, and he returned with herbs and plants, and she realized he'd made a poultice to prevent infection.

"We must perform a sing," Spirit Eagle said.

Sadie nodded at the idea of a healing ceremony. She took her place by Carter while Spirit Eagle began to chant. At the same time, he created a traditional Navajo sandpainting by trickling sand from his hand, sand made from fine grains of crushed pollen, cornmeal and charcoal from a burned tree to depict the Holy Ones.

When he was finished, Sadie left Spirit Eagle to apply the poultice, and she stepped outside the hogan. The night air felt hot and stifling, but she breathed it in, desperate to rid herself of the scent of Carter's blood and his near death.

"You were wonderful in there," Jimmy said quietly.

Sadie clenched her hands and glanced up at the moon and sky, willing her faith not to abandon her.

And praying that she had done enough to save Carter.

Chapter Twelve

Carter faded in and out of a deep and restless, pain-induced sleep, his mind bombarded with images of prison life, of beatings, then random images of endless miles of nothingness. Dried, dead shrub brush, cacti, desolate heat, roads that went nowhere, other roads that led into a dismal abyss that enveloped him into the darkness.

But occasionally the image of a beautiful wildflower interceded, a sea of purples and reds and yellows. Then there were vibrant Native American woven blankets and Indian beads, and Sadie's deep, dark, mesmerizing eyes.

During his foggy state, his fever spiked and he heard Sadie's worried voice talking to the medicine man. They'd carried him into some kind of sweatbox. Sadie had whispered in his ear, something about the heat cleansing his body and drawing out the poisonous toxins. That infection had set in, and his life depended on them ridding him of the toxins through a combination of herbal treatments and the sweathouse.

He had no idea if it was hours or days that he spent inside while the hot coals filled the small space with steam. His body shook and convulsed, perspiration pouring off him like a river. He passed in and out of a delusional state, dreaming about bizarre, dark forces coming for him.

And knowing he was all alone.

In those desolate, bleak hours, he yearned for Sadie's voice. For her touch. For a future with her.

Then confusion clouded his brain again. He had some place he needed to be. Something important he had to do.

He could not die until he finished that goal…

He had to save Sadie…

Clear his name…

The reality of the past crashed around him, and he jerked up, searching the darkness. The walls closed around him, the fire from the heat swirling in a cloudy haze.

Then voices floated to him from the outside.

A man's voice and a woman's.

"Sadie, you're an innocent in this situation," the man said. "Let me call the sheriff and we'll clear this up. If Flagstone is innocent like you claim, the police can sort out the mess."

"No, he tried the legal way before and it didn't work," Sadie said.

"But the cops are looking for you. They think you're an accomplice to murder," the man said gruffly. "You might go to jail—"

"I told you the truth about what happened," Sadie said. "I have to help Carter through this, Jimmy. I owe him that much."

"Why?" the man asked. "You could stay at the reservation and let me take care of you, Sadie."

A pause and he realized Sadie must be considering it. That this man meant something to her. That he wanted her.

"Jimmy," Sadie whispered. "I…can't."

"Why not? Don't tell me you're in love with that criminal?" Jimmy asked angrily. "That you'd throw away your future for a convicted felon?"

"I…Jimmy, I told you Carter is innocent," Sadie said in a low voice. "And I can't move on until this is over. I…feel too guilty."

Guilt. Carter understood about guilt. But he didn't want Sadie to risk her life for him. She was safe here.

Somehow he had to find a way to leave her at the reservation and finish the investigation on his own.

Even if he had to convince this guy Jimmy—

the man who obviously shared a past with Sadie and still loved her—to help him.

SADIE SHIFTED UNCOMFORTABLY under Jimmy's scrutiny, then pulled him away from the sweatbox. Carter had been unconscious for three days now. But she'd heard him stirring and hoped he hadn't overheard their conversation.

Jimmy rubbed her arm. "I just don't want to see you get hurt over some loser."

Sadie gritted her teeth. "He's not a loser, Jimmy. He's a good man. He just hasn't had any breaks in life."

"So you're making excuses for him?"

Anger flared inside Sadie. "No, I'm telling you the way it is. I'm the reason he went to jail for a crime he didn't commit. If I'd spoken up and testified, he wouldn't have been convicted. I have to fix it now."

"Then go to the police."

Sadie sighed. "You think they'd believe me? I'm on their wanted list."

A rumbling from across the plains made them both pause, and Sadie's stomach knotted as she spotted headlights in the distance. If anyone else discovered they were here, they might turn them in. "Who is that?"

Jimmy squinted through the darkness. "Jonas Buffalo. He's the head of the tribal police."

Sadie jerked her head toward Jimmy, betrayal gnawing at her. “You called him and told him we were here?”

Jimmy shook his head. “No. But the police have probably been investigating you. It won’t take them long to track you back to the reservation.”

Panic zinged through Sadie. “Carter and I have to leave.”

Jimmy caught her hand as she started to run back inside. “Don’t, Sadie. Stay and let me help you explain. We…” His voice thickened. “*I* need you around here. I miss you.”

Her anger melted at the concern in Jimmy’s eyes. But she knew he wanted more, a deeper relationship, and she had hurt him once before when she’d left. She couldn’t lead him on this time. “I’m sorry, Jimmy. But Carter and I have to find evidence to exonerate him first. Then we’ll go to the police.”

The SUV’s lights bounced over the hill, still a mile away but growing closer. Disappointment tinged Jimmy’s eyes for a brief second, but he gave a resigned nod. “There’s a storm cellar out back where you can hide in case Jonas insists on searching the hogan.”

Sadie stood on tiptoe and kissed him on the cheek. “Thanks, Jimmy. You’ve been a good friend.”

He frowned, then reached inside his pocket and handed her a key. "Take the old truck in the barn. The cops are looking for that station wagon."

In fact, he'd hidden it in the woods when they arrived.

She thanked him again, then rushed to Carter. He was trying to sit up and he looked weak, but some color had returned to his cheeks. The sweat-box seemed to have drawn out the infection, and his eyes looked clearer.

"We have to hide," Sadie said. "The tribal police are on their way."

Carter's eyes darkened to slits. "Your friend turned me in?"

Sadie shook her head and reached for his arm. "No, he's covering for us. Do you think you can stand?"

He pushed off the bed with his hand, but staggered slightly. Sadie slipped an arm beneath his to support him. "You're weak and need more rest," she said. "Hopefully the police will come and go."

"Just give me the keys to the car and I'll get out of here so you'll be safe," Carter said between gritted teeth.

"You can't drive now, Carter. You'd never make it."

His legs buckled, and she helped him into the

chair. "Sit here and let me make up the bed," she told him.

He glared at her, but did as she said, a testament to how weak he was. She hastily turned up the covers, then grabbed the bandages and medical supplies from the table and tucked them back inside the bathroom. If the police saw them, they might suspect Jimmy had treated Carter and arrest him.

She didn't want her friend to get in trouble.

Carter was gripping his bandaged belly, but he didn't complain. Instead, he accepted her help and shuffled his feet toward the back door as she led him outside. They paused for a second on the back stoop, and she heard the car engine slowing and rolling to a stop at the front of the house. Then a car door slammed shut and a man's deep voice punctuated the silence. "Jimmy?"

"Hey, Jonas. What brings you out here?" Jimmy asked.

Sadie gestured toward the right near a cluster of trees, and led Carter to the cellar door. She yanked it open and they crawled inside, then climbed down the steps into the darkness.

PAIN AND FATIGUE clawed at Carter, but at least his head felt more lucid, and he thought he was going to live. He didn't know how many days they'd been on the reservation, but it was time to leave.

Sadie pressed her hand to his forehead to check for a fever. "How are you feeling?" she whispered.

"Better." He gripped her arms. "Thanks for saving my life."

"No problem," she said softly.

Carter felt her body up against his, and a slow tingle of arousal pulsed through him. Yeah, he was alive.

But making love to Sadie was not an option. Not in a cellar with the cops on their tail. And not with his gut bandaged and him so weak a wave of dizziness washed over him.

Sadie must have sensed his condition because she urged him to sit down on the cold ground. He did, then leaned against the wall. The sound of his labored breathing echoed in the tense silence, and he watched helplessly as Sadie climbed the steps and listened for sounds above.

Somewhere Carter heard an owl hooting in the distance, then a dog barking. Finally the sound of an engine rumbling to life.

"He's leaving," Sadie said.

"Good. Then it's time I go, too." Using every bit of energy he could muster, he slowly pushed himself up, fighting the damn dizziness and hoping he didn't pass out again. He was a cowboy, not a weakling.

The noise above made him throw himself back against the wall into the shadows, and Sadie froze, her hand gripping the cellar door.

"It's me, Sadie," Jimmy called. "Jonas has gone."

Carter exhaled in relief, and Sadie released her grip on the door while her friend opened it, allowing a faint stream of moonlight to seep in.

"Come on, Carter."

He staggered to the stairway but insisted she exit first. When she'd made it through the clearing, she took his arm and helped him out. He was wheezing heavily, sweating like a racehorse and his mouth was so damn dry he felt like he'd been eating dust for days.

But he stifled a complaint as he faced Jimmy. The man obviously hated him. Had he tipped off the cops?

"What did Jonas say?" Sadie asked.

"The police paid him a visit asking about you, Sadie, if you were here."

Sadie cut her gaze toward the front of the house as if she, too, wondered if Jimmy had betrayed them. "What did you tell them?"

Jimmy stiffened. "That I hadn't heard from you. But that I'd let him know if you showed up."

A tense moment lingered between them, Jimmy's look possessive. Then Sadie squeezed his arm. "Thank you, Jimmy. I'm sorry for putting you in that position."

His eyes softened at her apology, confirming he was in love with Sadie.

"Thank you, Blackhorse." He cleared his throat. "If you'll hand me the keys, I'll get out of your way now."

Jimmy's gaze locked with his, a silent understanding passing between them. He had read Carter's double meaning, and he would take care of Sadie.

Sadie swung a startled look toward Carter. "We're leaving together, Carter."

Carter shook his head. "No. It's my battle, Sadie, not yours. Stay here where you'll be safe."

Sadie frowned. "No, Carter, I'm—"

"You've done all you can," Carter said, cutting her off. "I appreciate your help. But I don't need you now. I have to finish this on my own." He gestured toward Jimmy. "Stay here with your friend. He'll take care of you better than I can on the run."

Sadie's eyes flashed with anger. "That's not the point, Carter."

"Just give me the damn keys." He held out his hand. "And call the police after I'm gone and tell them I forced you to go with me. That I held you at gunpoint. Hell, you can even tell them about Lester. At least then they'll stop looking for you."

Jimmy shoved his keys in Carter's hand. "Take my old truck in the barn. They won't be looking for it."

Carter's stony gaze locked with Jimmy's, the tension palpable. But the men understood each other plain and clear.

They were both in love with Sadie, and would do whatever it took to keep her alive.

He glanced back at Sadie, fighting his baser instincts.

The urge to kiss her and tell her how he felt taunted him, but that would only complicate things more. Better she think he was done with her than to drag her along and get her killed.

So he headed toward the barn where Jimmy's truck was parked, forcing his mind back to Lester's comment about his father. If there was any truth in Lester's dying words, Carter would find out what it was.

SADIE WATCHED CARTER sway as he walked toward the barn, a mixture of emotions assaulting her. She should be relieved to be safe on the reservation and not on the run, but she couldn't let Carter go off on his own. The man was too weak to drive, could barely stand upright, much less fend off an attacker.

She turned to Jimmy. "Thanks again, but I have to go."

Sadness tinged his eyes, but he looked resigned. "Be careful, Sadie. I'll be here if you need me."

Sadie reached up and hugged him. He was such a good, honorable man, an advocate for their people, and had helped her after her own attack and through her mother's death. He deserved someone who really loved him.

But another man had stolen her heart. That stubborn cowboy who was about to leave her behind.

"Hang on and I'll go get your stuff," Jimmy said, then he raced back to the house.

Sadie caught Carter just as he entered the barn and reached for the door handle to the driver's side.

He whipped his head up, a bleakness in his eyes. "Sadie, go back—"

"No." She gripped his arm firmly. "You're too weak to drive. Now get in."

He shook his head but his eyes looked glassy. "No, stay—"

"Shut up and get in the car." Sadie tugged him around to the passenger side and gently shoved him in the seat. Then she hurried back to the driver's side, jumped in and took the keys from his trembling hand. Carter looked pale and shaky, so she stroked his forehead, checking for a fever.

"I'm fine," he grumbled, although his voice was hoarse.

A moment later, Jimmy pecked on the door, and she glanced up to see him holding the bags of clothing she'd purchased along with another bag, so she opened the door.

"I packed some extra gauze and ointment to dress his wounds and threw in some water and food."

"Thanks." Sadie stowed the bags behind her seat, removed a bottle of water and forced Carter to take a few sips, then waved to Jimmy and pulled from the barn.

"Why are you doing this?" Carter asked in a low voice.

Because I care about you. But Sadie swallowed back the confession teetering on the tip of her tongue and pressed the accelerator.

"I told you I want to know the truth," Sadie said. "Now where are we going?"

Carter pressed a hand to his bandaged stomach. "To my father's ranch first to pick up his computer and file box. Maybe there's some information there that will tell us who hired Lester."

"Then what? It's too dangerous to stay there."

"Then we'll go to the BBL. My friends will help us."

Sadie checked the horizon for the tribal police as she drove down the road leading away from Jimmy's and off the reservation.

Carter said his father had been mean, abusive. Was he so vile that he'd help frame his own son for murder?

And if so, why would he want his son to go to prison?

Chapter Thirteen

Darkness washed the deserted land with shadows, an occasional vehicle's lights flashing across the asphalt. Carter fought to stay awake as Sadie drove back to his father's ranch. She needed him to keep an eye out for the cops.

But fatigue and pain eventually wore him down, and he collapsed into a restless sleep.

Hours later, the truck jolted to a halt, and he jerked awake, then glanced around, his stomach churning as he realized they had made it back.

Sadie looked worn out, strands of her braid escaping the clasp, her shoulders sagging. "You look exhausted, Carter. Maybe we should stay here."

"No, you were right, it's too dangerous." He reached for the door handle. "I'll be right back."

Sadie jumped out of the truck and went around to help him. He leaned on her as they hurried into his father's office. A quick look around, and Carter grabbed the laptop, then the file box on the floor behind the desk.

A minute later, they were back in the truck heading to the BBL. Carter punched in Johnny's number to tell him they were coming.

"You can stay in the cabin next to Kim's," Johnny told him. "I'll come by tomorrow and we'll make a plan."

"Thanks, Johnny. I won't forget this." Carter ended the call, but fell asleep again as Sadie turned onto the highway.

The next time he roused, they were driving onto the BBL. Most of the ranch was dark, but they bypassed a campsite where a group of boys were huddled around a fire roasting marshmallows. Carter's chest tightened.

He admired the men who'd started the BBL. If he'd had a ranch like this to go to when he was a kid, he might not have landed himself in such trouble.

He gave Sadie directions to the cabin, and when they parked, she turned to him.

"Come on, let's get you to bed."

Carter caught her hand. "You need some rest, too, Sadie. You've been taking care of me day and night, and now you've driven for hours."

Sadie nodded. "We both need sleep, then we'll look at those files in the morning."

She opened the truck door, grabbed her purse and the water bottles and medical supplies her friend had packed for them, then walked around to the passenger side. Carter shoved open the door and tried to make it on his own, but his legs were weak, and blood had started oozing from his bandage.

Sadie frowned, then slid her arm around his waist and helped him inside. He collapsed into a kitchen chair, uncapped a water bottle and drank greedily while she stowed the groceries.

"Are you hungry?"

He shook his head. "No, but you must be."

"I'm fine. I ate a sandwich while you were sleeping."

She gestured toward his bandage, and he leaned back in the chair and sucked air through his teeth as she unwrapped the gauze, and cleaned and redressed the wound. Her fingers felt like magic, and his body hardened at her touch.

A good sign he wasn't dead and was healing.

"Let's go to bed," he said in a gruff voice.

Sadie's gaze met his, emotions brimming in her eyes. Then she stood, took his hand and helped him to the bedroom.

"Carter," she said hesitantly.

He cupped her face between his hands. "We're just going to sleep, Sadie. I promise." Dammit, he was too weak to do more. "I just want to hold you tonight."

A soft smile curved her tired face. "I'd like that, too."

Still shirtless, he sat down on the bed to remove his jeans. She helped him, his sex hardening again as she yanked off his boots then slid his jeans over his legs. Then she stepped into the bathroom, and returned a few moments later wearing one of the T-shirts she'd bought for him.

A dull ache pressed against Carter's chest. Dammit, he wanted her so badly he could taste it. But they were both exhausted.

Still, she was here. She had come with him when she could have stayed at the reservation with her friend Jimmy.

Maybe she was starting to care about him, too.

He stretched out, grimacing as his stitches pulled, then watched as she flipped off the light. A sliver of moonlight slanting through the window washed over her, making her look like an angel silhouetted by the light. She removed the clasp holding back her braid, then began to unwind the strands.

"Let me," he said hoarsely.

Sadie stared at him for a long moment, then walked over to the bed and sat down with her back to him. Tenderness for her mounted inside him as he lifted his fingers and threaded them through the silky strands of her hair. He gently unwove the braid, his pulse hammering as the beautiful, black strands fell across her bare shoulders.

He wanted the T-shirt off of her. Imagined what she'd look like naked with that hair spilling across his belly.

But he'd made her a promise and winning her trust meant more to him at this point than having sex with her. Although, even for an injured man, he wanted that desperately.

When he'd finished, he took her by the shoulders and gently urged her to join him in bed. Sadie slid her feet beneath the covers, then turned to him, her eyes bright with unshed tears.

"I'm not going to hurt you," he said gently.

She licked her lips, and he pulled her in his arms. She lay her head on his shoulder, one arm draped across his chest, and he wrapped her in his embrace, savoring the way her slender body fit against him.

He wanted to make love to her, but dammit, he was too weak to do anything but hold her. And he sensed that tonight, that was all she needed.

SADIE CURLED INTO Carter's strong embrace, anxiety needling her. They had to find the truth soon before the police caught up with them. She hadn't saved Carter's life after that bullet to lose him to jail or for him to be gunned down in an arrest.

But with Lester dead, where would they turn for answers? He still hadn't told them his motive.

Only that it was connected to Carter's father.

None of it made sense.

Carter brushed her hair from her forehead and kissed her cheek, and Sadie stroked his chest in small circles, enjoying the intimacy.

"You need rest," she whispered.

Carter nodded against her. "So do you."

Carter lifted her hand to his lips and kissed her fingers, feather-light kisses that aroused her with their tenderness. She twined her fingers with his, then kissed his palm, and he moaned and rolled sideways to tuck her against him.

She curled into his arms and closed her eyes. Seconds later, Carter's labored breathing echoed in the air. Knowing he still needed to heal, she savored the sound of his heartbeat against her ear. And while she lay entwined in his embrace, she imagined the two of them lying in bed together every evening, making love, holding each other, whispering promises long into the night. Then waking to sunlight streaking the room as they made love again in the morning.

Instead of the grueling reality they faced at daylight.

CARTER DREAMED HE WAS RUNNING from the police and they were shooting at him and Sadie. Then another man leaped out of the woods and shot Sadie.

The man was his father.

He wasn't dead after all. He had faked his disease, gone into hiding and helped frame Carter, and now he was determined to kill him before he exposed his father's duplicity.

He jerked awake, trembling and sweating and quickly turned to Sadie, terrified she was gone. But she lay curled on her side, her long dark hair spread across the pillow, a sliver of daylight streaking her skin as she slept.

He gently brushed his knuckles across her cheek, treasuring the moment. Thank God she was still alive and beside him.

He wanted her beside him all the time.

But what did he have to offer her?

Nothing.

His chest heaved with relief that she was safe, but he tensed again as remnants of his nightmare bombarded him. Could his father possibly still be alive?

Carter had only been told he'd died, first by an inmate, then by one of the low-life guards. Then he'd seen the obituary in the paper. But any of those things could have been faked or manipulated.

Carter assumed his body had been buried in

the old cemetery nearby, but he didn't know for sure. After all, he was a convicted murderer and he hadn't exactly bought a burial plot. He might even be buried somewhere on the ranch.

And no one had mentioned an autopsy.

For all he knew, his old man could have faked his death and come back to haunt him.

Tension thrummed through him as he searched the shadowed corners of the bedroom. He could be hovering in the dark watching him, waiting to strike like a rattlesnake ready to spew venom.

Just as Carter had learned to do in prison, he tempered his breathing, listening for sounds of an intruder in the room and throughout the house. The wind seeped through the eaves of the faded walls, whistling like an old man. The hum of the ceiling fan twirled above, rattling in the silence.

Sadie rolled over with a soft sigh and threw her arm above her head, making the shirt she was sleeping in ride up, revealing the soft skin of her thigh.

Dammit, he wanted her.

He shoved the covers aside and stood. His legs still felt a little unsteady, but he wasn't dizzy anymore, and he was actually hungry. That had to be a good sign.

He stumbled into the bathroom, took one look at his ragged beard stubble and sweat-soaked hair, and he flipped on the shower water, grabbed the toiletries Sadie had purchased for them, then shaved and showered.

Twenty minutes later, he bandaged his wound himself, feeling almost human again. Dressing in clean jeans and a T-shirt, he stepped into the kitchen, brewed a pot of coffee, then checked the refrigerator. Sadie's friend had given them some sandwiches, but she must have stopped at the store while he was passed out in the car because he found milk, eggs, sausage, cheese and butter. A loaf of bread and a jar of jelly also sat on the counter.

Elated to find something so normal as food that he could cook himself without having to eat in a prison, he pulled out the groceries, dropped a half dozen of the sausages into the frying pan and fried them, then cracked several eggs into a bowl, added milk and scrambled them. The coffee had finished dripping, so he poured himself a mug full and sipped it, listening for Sadie. She must have been exhausted, though, because she was still asleep, so he ate, then left the rest of the sausage and eggs for her and stepped onto the front porch of the cabin.

The sounds of the ranch bursting to life echoed in the air. Horses galloped across the pasture, cows were grazing, trucks firing up again. Then he heard the sound of boys across the way. He watched them enter the stables, then each one led a horse outside to the grooming stations. Déjà vu of his own days with Johnny and Brandon, when they'd managed to land stable boy jobs as young teens taunted him.

Two cowboys strode into the pen, then moved from one boy to the next instructing them. Emotions crowded his chest. The cowboys here really cared about these kids. Just like Johnny and Brandon did. He wished he was a part of it.

Maybe he could be one day. If he cleared himself…

Emboldened by that thought, he slipped back inside and booted up his father's computer.

A quick check and he noted that his father hadn't paid his bills online, so he turned to the file box and began searching through it. His father didn't have any kind of system, so he plowed through bills, past-due notices, truck repair invoices, out-of-date orders for feed and cattle, then sales receipts where he'd unloaded equipment to try to recoup losses before he'd gone to jail. He fished through another section and located foreclosure papers.

If his old man had let him take over, maybe he could have salvaged the ranch. But the SOB had refused to let Carter in the house.

Irritated, he yanked out several other folders and rifled through them. One in particular drew his eyes.

A letter from a man named Mulligan who had been interested in purchasing the ranch.

Mulligan—who the hell was he?

Another rancher? An investor?

His mind raced.

If someone wanted his father's ranch, what better way to obtain it than pick it up in foreclosure? The man could have bought it for next to nothing.

Especially with Carter out of the way in prison, unable to challenge a sale by claiming the property legally belonged to him.

He searched the folders but didn't find a bill of sale or any other connection to Mulligan. In the case of his father's death, he would have had to stipulate whom the property went to in his will.

If his old man even had one.

On a mission to find a will now, he thumbed through the remaining folders. Years of tax returns, bank statements, more bills he'd defaulted on…

A third of the way in, he hit pay dirt.

He found a brown manila envelope marked *Will,* so he removed it and opened the envelope. Itching to see if he was mentioned, he spread the document on the table and began skimming through the legal jargon.

But he stopped short when he reached the section about next of kin. Carter's name was nowhere to be found.

Instead, the will stipulated that the property go to a cousin of his, Elmore Clement.

Dammit, had his father hated him so much he'd rather give his land to a distant relative than to him?

To a cousin Carter had never even heard of?

SADIE ROLLED SIDEWAYS, feeling for Carter, but the bed was empty. A pang of disappointment enveloped her. She hadn't shared her bed with many men in her life, and even though she and Carter hadn't made love, she felt closer to him because he had held her in the night. In fact, it was the best night's sleep she'd had in years.

And for one night, she'd forgotten the danger and trouble following them.

Marginally refreshed, she rose and stepped into the bathroom. The scent of fresh soap and shampoo filled the room, indicating Carter had showered. He must be feeling stronger this morning.

Not knowing what they might face today, she stripped the nightshirt and stepped beneath the warm spray of water. As she shampooed her hair, she closed her eyes and imagined Carter joining her. She could see the water droplets glistening on his bare skin, his body hardening with desire as she reached out to stroke him.

Her body tingled, and she jerked her eyes awake. She never fantasized about a man. Especially not since the attack.

But she wanted more with Carter. She wanted him to touch her and erase the memory of Lester's brutal assault.

She wanted him to love her.

Dangerous territory.

Suddenly antsy to find out where he was and if he'd discovered a clue in the house, she rinsed and dried off, then hurriedly dressed. She couldn't find a hair dryer, so she braided her damp hair in a long braid to dry, then headed into the kitchen.

Carter was pouring a cup of coffee, a scowl on his face.

"What's wrong?" Sadie asked.

He handed her the mug, then poured another one for himself. "I found some papers that started me thinking."

Sadie settled into one of the kitchen chairs and sipped her coffee. "About what?"

Carter propped himself against the counter, his expression troubled. "First I found a letter from a man named Mulligan who was interested in buying my father's ranch."

"Mulligan?" Sadie said. "A man named Mulligan is overseeing the Uranium Mining Venture in Texas. Did your father sell to him?"

Carter shook his head. "No, at least I haven't found anything indicating that he did."

Sadie blew into the steaming mug. "You said you found something else?"

"Yes." Carter gestured toward the papers he'd spread on the table. "My father's will."

"He willed the land to you," Sadie said, hopeful.

Carter shook his head again. "Nope. To a cousin of mine I've never even heard of."

Sadie rubbed her temple in thought. "That sounds odd."

Carter tapped his foot. "Yeah, it does. My old man was not a family kind of guy. As a matter of fact, I don't remember him ever mentioning any relatives. His parents died before I was even born. He had no siblings that I know of. So who is this cousin?"

Sadie frowned, sensing his suspicions. "You think someone forged the papers?"

"It occurred to me." Carter shrugged. "Just think about it. My father gets locked up. Someone wants this land, and my dad's sick. Maybe he's on drugs or on his deathbed and they con him into signing a will where they've altered the beneficiary." He snapped his fingers. "Come to think of it, maybe he didn't die of natural causes. Maybe they murdered him for the land."

"And with you in prison, no one is around to question it," Sadie said, following his logic.

Carter's frown grew deeper. "That's right. And we both know someone set me up."

Sadie sighed. "To get you out of the way."

"Right." Carter paced to the table and straddled a chair. "Now I just have to figure out why they wanted the land bad enough to frame me for murder."

Sadie's head swam. If Carter was right, they were still in danger.

And if Lester had been working for someone else, whoever that was wouldn't stop until they covered up the past and killed Carter.

A knock sounded at the door, and they both tensed.

Chapter Fourteen

Carter reached for his weapon and motioned for Sadie to go into the bedroom, but before she could make it, the door opened.

Johnny poked his head in. Surprise tightened his face at the sight of Carter's gun.

"Dammit, Johnny," Carter mumbled. "I could have shot you."

"Sorry." Johnny shut the door and stepped inside. "I told you I'd come by this morning and we'd make a plan."

"I know," Carter mumbled. "I'm just on edge."

He gestured toward Sadie and introduced them, then explained what he'd found so far, reiterating his theory.

If someone wanted his father's ranch and wanted it cheap, what better way than to pick it up in foreclosure? Whoever had orchestrated this plan must have known that Carter would have dropped everything to run the place and keep it afloat.

"So sending you to jail for murder paved the way for them to sneak in and finagle the land away from your father," Johnny said. "Sounds like a drastic plan to obtain control of land that might not be worth anything."

"Maybe it was worth more than we thought," Carter said.

"He could be right," Sadie added. "Mulligan, the man who was interested in buying his land, works for the Uranium Mining Venture. The tribal community has dealt with him before. He's really pushing mining in the state."

"I heard about him," Johnny said tightly.

Sadie scowled. "The Navajo community has been worried about uranium mining and its effect on their only water source. In the late '70s, Navajo uranium miners and their families asked for help to prove that their lung diseases had been caused by their work in underground mines from the '40s to the '60s."

Carter jerked his head up. "Lung diseases?"

Sadie nodded. "Congress adopted legislation in 1990 to compensate former miners and their survivors." Sadie made a frustrated sound. "But it's not enough. There were so many people affected by it, it's been difficult to process all the complaints. Who knows how it will affect future generations, especially if standards are not instigated to protect the water supply."

Carter's suspicions mounted. His father had developed lung cancer. "Sadie, this may be the clue we've been looking for."

Johnny frowned. "Dammit, if they are mining that land it could be affecting our water supply on the BBL, too. Lately, we'd discovered some small animals dead. And yesterday, Brody reported a couple of our cows were sick."

"Then the venture has to be stopped," Carter said.

Sadie stood and made a sandwich with the sausage, cheese and toast. "Carter, how did your father die?"

"They told me he had lung cancer." He pulled his hand down his chin. "But now I'm wondering what really happened."

Johnny drummed his fingers on the table. "There are mines on your daddy's property, Carter. Remember, we used to play out near them when we were little."

"Yeah, I don't know if they have uranium in them, though."

"They must, or Mulligan wouldn't have been interested. With the need for U.S. uranium nuclear energy products, that land is probably really valuable."

Carter's stomach knotted. "Enough so that someone might have killed to gain access to it."

SADIE SEARCHED HER MEMORY for details about Mulligan. He was a cutthroat businessman who went after what he wanted and got it.

He must have discovered that Carter's ranch land was valuable. But would he frame Carter for murder to get him out of the way so he could gain access to it?

"But how does Dyer fit into the puzzle?" Sadie asked.

"Maybe he was working for Mulligan," Carter suggested.

"That's a possibility." The controversy at the reservation over the water issues had been going on for years. Growing up, she remembered losing several of the elders to lung cancer after watching them wither away.

If Mulligan was prospering because of it and continuing to mine without following standards, he had to be stopped. And if it affected the BBL, they were not only endangering animals but also the kids and employees of the BBL.

"I have to find this so-called cousin of mine," Carter said. "See if he's behind this."

"Where is he?" Johnny asked.

Carter glanced at the papers in search of an address and frowned. "The address is for an office in San Antonio. I'm going there to find him. Maybe he can verify if there are uranium mines on the Flagstone farm."

Sadie shrugged. "We could go look for them ourselves."

"We will, but the ranch is a big piece of property. First I want to confront Elmore Clement and see how he convinced my father to list him as his beneficiary."

"How can I help?" Johnny asked.

"See what your P.I. friend can dig up on Dyer, Mulligan and Clement."

Johnny gave a clipped nod. "You got it."

Carter gripped his side as he stood. "By the way, where is my dad buried?"

"The old cemetery near his property."

"Did they do an autopsy?" Carter asked.

Johnny shrugged. "I don't know. You want me to find out?"

"Yeah, and if they didn't do one, see if we can have his body exhumed and get one done."

"That's not an easy feat," Johnny said. "You'll need a court order, and no judge is going to issue one unless he has evidence of a suspicious death."

Carter gritted his teeth. "Then we find evidence."

Sadie stood. "Let's go, Carter."

Carter dumped the rest of his coffee, then

opened the door and the three of them headed outside.

Maybe Carter would finally find the answers he deserved.

ADRENALINE RACED through Carter. He finally felt as if he was close to the truth.

And as he watched the boys grooming the horses on the way past the stable, fierce protective instincts kicked in.

These kids needed the BBL, and he wasn't about to let someone endanger them or the animals here.

"Are you thinking that cancer didn't kill your father?" Sadie asked.

"I don't know," Carter said. "He was obviously sick, but maybe someone helped him to an early grave so they could gain access to his land."

Had his father known about the mines? Or had he actually been part of the scheme, then victimized?

Dammit. His father had been such a low-life bastard it was hard to believe he'd ever been victimized, or that someone could have cheated him.

But Carter hadn't seen him in years, and disease and years of booze could rob a man of his mind.

Carter scanned the roads and side roads, searching for cops as they headed into San Antonio.

Early morning traffic was starting to thicken, and Sadie tried to blend in, weaving into traffic with the daily commuters.

"What's the address?" Sadie asked.

He read her the street number, absentmindedly patting the will inside his pocket. He knew it was risky to confront Clement himself, but it was a risk he had to take. Besides, he wanted to see Clement's reaction, if he'd already drawn up papers to transfer the deed to himself. Or maybe he'd already sold the property to Mulligan.

Most likely, Clement was a con man, and he and Mulligan had been working together from the beginning.

Sadie maneuvered through the downtown streets of San Antonio, past the riverfront, then down a side street on the other side of the city.

"We're leaving San Antonio," Sadie said. "Are you sure this address is correct?"

Carter frowned. "That's what it said in the documents. Clement supposedly worked for a real estate agency." She veered down the highway a few miles until they came to a set of smaller buildings, some that looked abandoned, as if the strip had once held businesses but they had all gone defunct.

"That's the address."

She turned into the parking lot, and he checked

the numbers. A sagging real estate sign teetered in the wind advertising the entire strip was for sale. Overgrown shrubs and dry, brittle grass bordered the ramshackle building. Two had been boarded up while the windows had been knocked out in the middle unit, and graffiti littered the front of the last building on the right. The real estate office.

"It doesn't look like anyone's been here in a long time," Sadie said.

"Maybe, maybe not." Carter opened the truck door. "Could be the reason Clement used it. They wanted an out-of-the-way meeting site that wouldn't create suspicion."

Sadie shrugged, climbed out and walked beside him to the last building on the left. The wooden steps creaked as they climbed the stoop, then Carter checked the door to see if it was locked. But the door screeched open, and a strange feeling swept through Carter as if they were entering a ghost town.

Then the vile stench hit him. Human wastes. Blood. Body decay.

Sadie gagged and rocked back on her heels, stepping back outside to drag in air. Carter yanked a handkerchief from his pocket and covered his nose and mouth.

"Wait out here, Sadie. And yell if you see a car."

Sadie clenched the door edge, her mouth twisting into a grimace. "It smells like death."

"I know. I have a bad feeling it's Clement."

Sadie gripped his arm. "Be careful."

He gave her a clipped nod, then inched inside. Cobwebs and mold added to the weathered feeling, the sight of dried blood on the floor confirming his suspicions about the source of the smell.

He crept closer, scanning the dark hallway from the front reception area to the back room where the odor was coming from. One step at a time, he moved, listening in case someone else appeared, but judging from the odor, whoever was dead had been dead for a while. Flies and insects buzzed, the stench of body fluids evident.

Seconds later, he found a man lying in a pool of dried blood and brain matter. He had been shot in the head.

Cursing, Carter stooped down and checked his pocket. He found a wallet, then removed the ID. He was right. Elmore Clement. Fifty-five years old. Texas resident. Real estate license.

Dammit, he sure as hell couldn't tell Carter what had happened.

His nerves suddenly kicked up a notch. Was he being set up again?

He paused to listen for the cops, then jumped into action and searched the desk, hoping to find some lead to Mulligan or to his father and his ranch. But the desk drawer was empty and so was the filing cabinet. Then he spotted a shredder filled with shredded paperwork and realized whoever had killed Clement had covered up by destroying a paper trail that might lead back to them.

Carter clenched his hands into fists. He wanted to pound out his frustration. So far everyone associated with the past—Dyer, Lester, Loretta Swinson and now Clement—was dead. Which led back to Mulligan.

He was the only lead left.

Another suspicion nagged at him. What if the will had been forged, even planted at the ranch for the cops to find? When they discovered Clement dead, they'd assume Carter had killed the man to recover his land.

And dammit, his fingerprints were on the desk and Clement's wallet.

Irritated with himself, he wiped down the desk, the filing cabinet drawers, then took the wallet with him. Sadie was still on the porch, her face pinched in worry.

He wiped the doorknob, then grabbed her hand. "Come on, we have to get out of here."

SADIE FASTENED HER SEAT BELT, the stench of the dead man's odor still lingering in her nose. "You think whoever killed him plans to frame you for this murder, too?"

"I don't know, but I'm not taking any chances." Carter shifted into gear and drove from the parking lot back through San Antonio.

"Maybe you should contact the police and fill them in on what you've discovered, Carter. Surely they'll listen now and investigate."

"I have to find proof of the mines before I can even think about turning myself in."

"Then we search for the mines," Sadie said.

Carter swung his gaze toward her, his eyes boring into hers. "You know you can leave anytime, Sadie. Go to the cops and explain what Lester did. Tell them I forced you to go with me."

"No, then they'll add kidnapping charges to your record." Sadie twined her fingers with his. He'd offered her a way out more than once now. But she didn't intend to abandon him. Not this time.

"I'm with you," she said softly. Besides, she owed it to her people and the kids on the BBL to investigate. If mines were being excavated without protective environmental measures, both the reservation's and the BBL's water supplies could be adversely affected. She had to expose the truth.

Carter studied her for a long moment, emotions darkening his eyes, then he turned his attention back to the road, and they lapsed into a strained silence. When they reached the ranch, Carter passed the farmhouse, taking back roads and side roads in search of the mines.

They checked the east quadrant, then the west, then drove south, scanning the flatland and the ridges. The sun slanted across the horizon, beating down on the dry, parched land.

Sadie spotted a dip in the land and something that looked like it might have been a shovel. "Over there."

Carter veered down the graveled road, his jaw clenched as he ground to a halt. They both climbed out and walked over to examine the mine, and Carter stooped to look at the tools left in the dirt.

"Primitive, but someone has been digging around." He retrieved a flashlight from the truck, then gestured toward the entrance.

"I'm going inside. Wait here and keep watch."

Sadie nodded and watched as he disappeared inside the cave. The hot sun blazed down, and perspiration beaded on her skin as she waited. It seemed like hours before he finally returned.

"No evidence of active mining, but it looks like someone's definitely been snooping around." He gestured toward the truck. "I want to take a look at the mines where I played as a kid."

Sadie climbed back in the truck and drove three miles down the road. Old mining equipment, tools and footprints indicated someone had been working this area recently, too.

Carter shined the flashlight around the entrance, and Sadie once again waited outside to keep watch.

A half hour later, Carter still hadn't returned. Sadie paced, anxious, and was starting to get worried, so she poked her head inside.

"Carter?"

An engine rumbled in the distance, and she glanced toward the west end and spotted an SUV racing over the hill. Her nerves instantly jumped to alert. She had to warn Carter that someone was coming.

Frantic, she ducked inside the dark mine, chilled at the change in temperature as she tried to adjust her eyes. "Carter?"

He didn't answer, alarming her more, so she felt along the sides of the mine and noted workers had erected support beams. She stumbled over a rock jutting from the ground and almost tripped over some tools that had been left on the ground, then inched deeper into the cave.

"Carter?"

"Sadie?"

Footsteps clattered ahead, and she hurried

toward them. Outside the engine grew louder before it shut off. “Carter, someone’s coming. An SUV.”

The sound of rocks tumbling along the wall of the mine echoed in the silence, then a car door slammed.

“Carter, where are you?”

“Back here. Stay there, I’m coming.”

But before she found him, a loud explosion rent the air. It took Sadie a moment to realize what had happened, then the mine walls and ground shook, rocks and dirt rained down on top of her, pelting her. She covered her head with her arms and dropped to the ground, dodging debris as the mine collapsed around her.

Chapter Fifteen

Sadie's scream echoed through the mine as the mine walls collapsed. Carter took off at a dead run, shining the flashlight through the dark tunnel and debris as dust, rocks and dirt pummeled him.

"Sadie!"

He paused to listen, dodging a chunk of rock, then pressed himself against the wall as part of the ceiling caved in. Blinking to clear dust from his eyes, he peered through the foggy interior, hoping Sadie had survived and made it outside.

But his gut pinched with worry at the fact that she hadn't answered him when moments before he'd heard her calling his name.

He panned the flashlight across the interior of the mine, cursing when he saw the mounds of dirt and rock. A narrow opening loomed ahead, not big enough to get through. He'd have to dig his way to Sadie and hope that the rest of the mine didn't collapse on top of him.

Wondering if he should try to find another way

out, he swept the flashlight behind him, searching the darkness. But if Sadie was trapped inside, he had to go back. He couldn't leave her there. She might die from suffocation.

And nothing mattered to him more than Sadie.

She had come inside to warn him that she'd heard someone outside. Had that person triggered the explosion to kill them?

Anger fueled his energy, and he propped the flashlight on the ground at an angle to give him a view of the tunnel, then found a sharp rock and used it to dig through the mound. He tossed dirt behind him, careful to leave an opening for him and Sadie to escape the other side if they needed. He worked diligently for the next half hour, digging his way through the dirt and rock, yelling Sadie's name as he inched his way back toward the entrance.

He felt along the walls, his anger renewed as he recalled the equipment he'd discovered, and the evidence of recent excavation activities. Who had been working the mine?

The person who'd framed him and wanted him and Sadie dead?

Carter spit out dirt and cursed. The bastard wouldn't get away with it. He would see to that.

"Sadie!" he yelled. "If you're in here, answer me."

A low moan reverberated from somewhere up ahead, the brittle sound making his throat catch.

"I'm coming, darlin'," he said, as much to reassure himself as to assure her that he wouldn't let her down.

He clawed his way through the next few feet of dirt, forcing himself to take shallow breaths to conserve the air, and slid on his belly through the narrow space he'd cleared.

He finally dropped to a wider opening and swept the flashlight across the space, then spotted Sadie lying on the ground, half-covered in dirt.

His heart pounded with worry and fear as he crawled toward her. "Sadie, honey, tell me you're okay."

She moaned again, and he checked her pulse, then searched her for injuries.

"Sadie, I'm here, honey. It's all right."

"Carter?" Her throaty whisper echoed with fear. "I…tried to warn you…someone's out there."

"I know," he said between gritted teeth. "He probably set the explosion to trap us inside." He stroked her hair from her cheek and gently rolled her over, searching her face. "Are you hurt?"

She coughed, straining for a breath, then winced as she tried to sit up. "No…just bruised."

He felt along her neck, then her abdomen. "Are you sure? Are you in pain?"

Sadie clenched his hand. "I'm okay. It just knocked the wind out of me."

His pulse clamored with relief, and he dragged her in his arms and clung to her, rocking her back and forth. He didn't realize how terrified he'd been that she was hurt, that he might lose her.

He didn't like the feeling or want to experience it again.

But he couldn't help himself. He held her tight.

The only thing he cared more about than clearing his name was keeping Sadie alive.

SADIE WAS TREMBLING as Carter cradled her in his arms. She'd been desperately afraid he'd been killed in the explosion, trapped so deep in the mine that she'd never reach him, and that she'd never be able to dig her way out.

She buried her head in his arms. "I was so afraid I'd lost you," she whispered.

"I was scared, too," he admitted in a raw whisper. "But they're not going to stop us, Sadie. We're going to get to the bottom of this."

Sadie nodded against his chest. "Yes, we are."

He pulled back to look at her, and cupped her face between his hands. "Are you really okay?"

In spite of her fear and the fact that they were trapped in the mine with little air, knowing that he still had fight left gave her a surge of energy. "Yes. And you're right—we're not giving up."

He blew out an exasperated breath. "Did you see who was driving up?"

She shook her head. "No, it was a dark SUV. I ran inside as he was racing down the hill."

Carter stroked her hair from her face. "He's probably still outside, so we need to find an alternate escape."

"How far did you go in the mine?"

"A few hundred feet," he said. "It's definitely being mined. But that means there may be another way out. Come on, we'll crawl through the tunnel I dug, then hunt for an escape."

Sadie nodded and clung to him, trusting him with all her heart.

And hoping that he was right, that there was another exit. Otherwise, they might die in here.

And no one would ever know where they were or what had happened to them.

CARTER DROPPED TO HIS KNEES and crawled on his belly back through the tunnel, leading the way for Sadie. Inch by inch, he slid until he crept through the opening to the section where he'd been when the explosion had occurred. His belly ached, and he hoped to hell he hadn't busted open his stitches, but he didn't have time to think about it.

He took a deep breath as he entered the wider

opening, then reached out to pull Sadie the rest of the way through. Dirt streaked her cheek and hair as she stood and brushed off her skirt, but she looked so damn beautiful, and he was so grateful she was alive, that he couldn't resist pulling her into his arms again.

Sadie curled into them as if she belonged, and he held her close, savoring her breath fanning his cheek as she lifted her face to his.

"What do we do now?"

The tenuous tremor in her voice made his protective instincts surge to life. "Let's follow the tunnel. There has to be an opening at the other end."

Sadie nodded. "Then let's find it. Maybe we can catch whoever was outside."

Determination kicked in. "You're damn right we're going to."

Carter flipped the flashlight to the path ahead and shined it along the walls and floor. Then he took Sadie's hand as they wove through the tunnel.

"You're right. Someone was working this mine," Sadie said as they passed equipment and more support beams that had been erected.

"Yeah, I just wonder who's behind it, and if my father knew."

Carter struggled for a breath, but the dust and

cramped space seemed to be sucking the air from them. They twisted and turned through the dark maze, following one turn that led to a dead end. They had to regroup and head back in the opposite direction.

Finally they reached a clearing and Carter detected sunlight filtering through a tiny opening. "There's light ahead. Even if there isn't an exit, we can make one."

"Should we go back and get some of those tools?"

"I'll go." Carter squeezed her arm to assure her he'd be back, but suddenly another explosion rocked the earth, this time up ahead, and dirt and rocks crashed down in front of them. The walls seemed to slide away as the ground trembled, and dust engulfed them.

Sadie screamed, and he pulled her into his embrace, dragging her back against the wall. He pulled her down to the ground, then covered her head and body with his arms to protect her from the falling rocks.

They huddled together, dodging more dirt and stones until the earth stopped shaking and the rocks settled in a pile a few feet from them. Sadie coughed against him, and he released her long enough to see if she was okay.

"Sadie?"

"I'm all right. Are you?"

He breathed out in relief. "Yeah, just pissed off."

Sadie surprised him by emitting a low laugh.

"That's funny?" he growled.

She looked up at him with a mixture of worry and fear. "No, but I'm glad you're here with me."

Carter's chest ached. He had never been in love with a woman before, and he felt crazy with it now.

Stupid. Like he was hot and cold at the same time. Happy but scared out of his mind.

Stupid like he wanted to tell her that he'd always be with her.

And that was crazy.

They were trapped in a damn mine and might not make it out alive.

SADIE KNEW THEIR SITUATION was critical, that they could easily die in this hellhole. Or, if the killer was waiting outside, they could walk into an ambush.

Meaning they should lay low for a little while. Let him think they died.

"I'll get us out of here," Carter said in a gruff voice. "I promise."

Sadie nodded. "I trust you, Carter."

The flashlight was burning low, but she could still see the emotions tingeing his eyes. Trust was obviously not something he was accustomed to receiving—or giving.

And neither was love.

More rumbling started, rocks sliding and skittering around them, and Carter pulled her to him again. Dirt scattered around them, robbing her breath, then the darkness swallowed them, closing them in.

A shudder ripped up Sadie's spine. Carter's determination to save them gave her hope, but there was a chance they wouldn't survive.

And she didn't want to die without being with Carter one more time. Without showing him her love and proving to herself that he had made her whole again.

So she slid her hands into his hair and drew him to her for a kiss. Carter heaved a breath, then closed his mouth over hers, greedily taking what she offered, a hungry sound ripping from his throat.

"I want you, Carter," Sadie whispered. "Please. I need you to hold me and make me feel alive."

Carter cupped her face between his hands. "We will get out of here, Sadie. I swear."

Sadie nodded, then pressed a kiss to the base of his throat, savoring the salty taste of his skin and the hum of arousal that rumbled from his chest.

"God, Sadie, do you know how long it's been?"

"A long time for me, too," she whispered.

He wound his arms around her, nipping at her neck. "I should be digging our way out now."

"We'll do it together, but he may be waiting to kill us if we show ourselves," Sadie said softly. "And right now, I need to be close to you."

Carter paused, then lowered his mouth to hers, hovering an inch from her lips. "Are you sure, Sadie? This is not the most romantic place—"

"We're together and I need you. That's romantic enough for me."

Carter groaned, then seemed to give in and claimed her mouth with an intensity that robbed her breath. His tongue probed her lips apart, seeking, yearning, exploring. Moved by his touch, she threaded one hand in the thick, wavy strands of his hair, trailing the other one down his jaw, then to his chest and lower, until he wrapped his leg around her and pressed his erection against her belly.

Sadie had never felt anything more erotic in her life. She stroked his calf with her foot, then tore at his shirt with her fingers, ripping it off. Her hand connected with his bandage, and she froze.

"Carter…I forgot. I don't want to hurt you."

"Are you kidding?" he said in a deep, sexy rumble that bordered on pain and joy at the same time. "You have no idea how many nights I fantasized about being with you again. It was the only thing that kept me alive in prison."

Sadie tensed for a moment, knowing he'd also fantasized about killing her, but they had moved past that point, and she trusted him now with her heart, her soul, her body.

With her love.

Because she was totally in love with Carter Flagstone. The renegade cowboy, the felon, the man who'd risked his life to save hers more than once.

So she invited his touch, and when he slowly stripped her clothes and his jeans, then spread his clothes on the ground to make a bed for them, she lay naked and waiting, welcoming him between her legs.

Hunger spiraled through her, heating her blood to a frenzy as he dipped his head to taste one nipple, then he suckled her deep and hard, first one then the other until she cried out his name and felt herself coming apart in his arms.

HUNGER FUELED Carter's energy as he felt the first strains of Sadie's orgasm rippling through her. He wanted more.

Wanted to sink himself inside her until she forgot all the pain in the past and remembered only the pleasure that he could give her.

She clawed at his back, urging him to make

love to her, and he eased himself on top of her, carefully bracing himself so as not to crush her. Before, she'd felt smothered—he didn't want to smother her now.

Only envelop her in his love.

"Carter?" she whispered into the darkness.

"I'm here, Sadie, I'm right here." He lowered his mouth to hers again, seeking, taking, telling her with his tongue what he intended to do with his body. She parted her legs for him, an invitation that spiked his blood, and he thrust his hips against hers, stroking her heat until she moaned and wrapped her fingers around his thick length.

He throbbed in her hands, aching to be inside her, and she guided him to her warm chamber, urging him to fill her. Gritting his teeth to keep from shouting, he plunged inside her, the slow burn of release teetering on the edge of exploding.

He wanted to stall the moment, but it had been five long years since he'd felt the loving caress of a woman, and Sadie was the woman he'd always wanted.

"I love you, Carter."

Her whispered words tore at his heart as he thrust again and lost himself inside her.

Sadie clung to him, crying out his name as she came again, and he kissed her soundly, then rolled to his side and swept her in his arms, tucking her head into the crook of his shoulder as he tried to make sense of the strange emotions overcoming him.

Sadie had said she loved him.

Had she only muttered the words in the heat of the moment?

Of course she had. He was a two-bit cowboy, a convicted felon with nothing to offer her. He had dragged her into a mess, had almost gotten her killed, and he still wasn't sure he could keep his promise and get them out of here alive.

But he would die trying, dammit.

Adrenaline shot through him and he suddenly pulled away, sat up and reached for his clothes. Sadie pressed her hand to his back.

"Come here, Carter."

Tension knotted his shoulders, though, as he realized time was of the essence. He had no idea how much air they had left. And it wasn't like anyone was actually looking for them. No one except the cops.

And he'd done his best to keep them from knowing where he was.

He yanked on his jeans and shirt and boots, then grabbed the flashlight. "I'm going back a few feet and see if I can find one of those picks or shovels."

Sadie sat up and wrapped her arms around herself. He glanced down, aching to lie back down and make love to her again. But if they died or he went back to jail, he'd never get the chance.

"Carter, let me go with you," Sadie said.

"No, I'll be right back." He didn't wait for a response, but rushed back through the tunnel, shoving rocks and sticks aside to find the area where the miners had left their tools. Time felt suspended, and worry nagged at him. His ears were honed, listening for another explosion. Finally the flashlight beam caught the tools half-buried in the rubble, and he scooped away enough dirt with his hands to uncover a shovel, then rushed back toward Sadie.

By the time he reached her, she was dressed and combing the area for a way out.

"The light was coming from that direction," he told her.

She didn't comment, and for a moment he sensed he'd done something wrong, but he didn't have time to analyze it. He had to get them out.

So he propped the flashlight on the ground at an angle, grabbed the shovel and pick and began to work. Sadie joined him a minute later, taking the pick from him and hacking away at the wall of dirt and rock that had fallen.

By the time they dug through the collapsed debris and crawled through to an opening, they were sweaty and filthy. He spotted the sliver of light from a few feet above, and gestured for Sadie to help him move the dirt surrounding it, hoping to make a clearing to free them.

"Be careful," Carter said. "We could bring the whole damn cave down."

She gave him a small nod, then worked more gently, prodding the soil nearest the opening to test it before she continuing hacking.

They worked diligently until they'd made a hole large enough for Carter to see a way out. "Step back and let me finish," he said, his heart drumming. "The mine's roof could collapse any minute."

And what if they crawled out and walked into a trap?

Hell, it was a chance he had to take.

He felt for the gun inside his jacket, grateful he still had it.

Then he spun around toward Sadie. "I'll go first and see if it's safe."

Sadie reached for him, cradled his face and kissed him passionately. When he pulled away, he stroked her cheek gently for a brief second, then removed his gun and held it at the ready as he dragged himself through the hole.

Fresh air and the waning sunlight drenched the wooded area where the mine spilled out. He scanned the area, listening for sounds of the man who'd set off the explosion, then saw something running in the distance. A deer? A bobcat?

The man?

Fueled by rage and the need to catch the culprit, he pulled himself the rest of the way out.

"Carter?"

He reached down and offered Sadie a hand. "Come on, Sadie. I think it's okay."

Suddenly footsteps crunched dried leaves and grass, and bushes rustled.

Then the shadow of a man lumbered over him.

Carter froze as the man shoved the barrel of a gun in his face.

Chapter Sixteen

"Move, cowboy, and you're dead."

Carter gritted his teeth as he stared into the condemning eyes of Sheriff Otto. The man who had been sheriff before McRae, the same man who had arrested him for Dyer's murder. "How did you find me, Otto?"

He grunted. "I figured you'd eventually end up here." He cocked the gun and Carter tensed.

Barring assaulting an officer, he had no way out. Resigned, he held up his hands in surrender. "Don't shoot. Just listen to me, and let me get the woman down there out."

The sheriff's ruddy face curled into a snarl. "The woman whose been helping you escape?"

"She's innocent," Carter said emphatically. He gripped her hand, then helped her through the opening.

Sadie collapsed on the ground, knees pulled up, gasping for air. "You have to listen to us," Sadie said, her eyes widening as she spotted the sheriff's weapon trained on them. "Someone framed Carter for murder and we know the reason. We can prove it. He tried to kill us."

Carter cleared his throat, slowly standing to face the sheriff, determined to draw the man's gun away from Sadie. "It has to do with my father's ranch," Carter explained. "Dyer was working for a man named Mulligan. Mulligan is head of the Uranium Mining Venture in the state. Somehow he discovered uranium mines on my father's property and knew they could make a fortune by mining them if they owned the ranch. But they needed my father and me out of the way."

"So Dyer used me," Sadie said. "He threatened to kill me if I didn't help him frame Carter."

Carter started to wipe sweat from his eyes, but the sheriff tightened his grip on the gun and kept it aimed at him, so he forced himself to remain still. "Someone in cahoots with Mulligan, maybe Elmore Clement, killed Dyer to frame me, then sent Clement to con my father into signing his ranch over to him."

"I know about Clement," the sheriff said, his voice cracking. "He was your cousin, but you killed him, too, when you learned your father willed him the ranch."

"I didn't kill him," Carter said. "And he's not my cousin. He's a con man."

The sheriff arched a thick, bushy brow. "You have it all figured out, don't you?"

The hairs on the back of Carter's neck stood on end. "Not everything. I'm not sure Mulligan was running the show, but he's a place to start."

A sinister bark of laughter rumbled from the sheriff's chest. Sadie shivered at the sound, and Carter tensed, his pulse drumming.

"You're not as smart as you think," the sheriff said. "And you aren't getting off."

Carter's gut tightened. "I know enough to have my case reopened," he said. "To start a new investigation."

"That's not going to happen." The sheriff waved his gun toward Sadie, then back at him. "You're not going back to jail, either."

"Then you're going to help us?" Sadie asked.

Carter's suspicions mounted at the sound of the sheriff's bark of laughter.

"I'm helping you, all right." The sheriff grabbed Sadie's arm. "Out of my way and into your grave."

SADIE GASPED and tried to yank her arm away, but the sheriff shoved her back toward the mine opening. "What are you doing? You're a lawman. You're supposed to help us."

Carter fisted his hands beside him. "Let her go, Otto."

Sheriff Otto shook his head. "No way. I've

made it this far. And you sure as hell aren't going to stop me now."

"What?" Sadie whispered.

"He's behind it all," Carter said, his tone dark but matter-of-fact, as if the pieces had finally clicked into place. "How did you find out about the uranium mines?"

Otto tugged at his belt. "I lived in these parts all my life. I knew the area might have some mines. When Mulligan started asking around, I did a little search of my own. Then your daddy got out of jail and started spoutin' off that he was gonna make him a fortune before he died."

Sadie's head reeled from shock.

"So you helped him along," Carter said. "And what about Clement—you set him up to do your dirty work, then killed him to keep him quiet?"

"Dyer and Clement were both losers." Sheriff Otto shook his head, shifting and rubbing at his leg. "Ex-cons come in handy sometimes."

Sadie shivered. No wonder Carter had been framed so easily. The sheriff had ties and had easily planted evidence against Carter.

Carter narrowed his eyes. "So you killed Clement and Loretta Swinson, too."

Otto made a clicking sound with his teeth. "Like I said, nothing is going to stop me. Your daddy was a mean bastard and didn't deserve that money." He waved the gun back and forth between them, a crazed look in his eyes. "But me, I done good all my life."

"You've killed three, four people so far," Carter growled. "And now you plan to kill two more."

"Being good didn't pay off." The burly man cocked the gun then grabbed Sadie's arm again.

"You can't do this," Sadie said. "Think of the innocent women and kids on the reservation and the BBL. They deserve safe water."

He waved the gun at Sadie.

"Enough talk. Get back in there. Now."

He flung Sadie into the entrance, and she cried out as her knees hit jagged rock. Carter lunged at the sheriff with a vicious snarl.

They both flew backward against a tree, then the gun went off, the shrill sound muffled by Carter's grunt of pain.

Panic zinged through Sadie. Had Carter been shot again?

PAIN SLAMMED INTO CARTER, but he managed to dodge the bullet. Still Otto had hit him in his gut where he'd been shot before, and blood trickled from his belly.

Sadie screamed behind him. Fury enraged him, fueling his energy, and he jerked Otto's gun hand up. Otto squeezed the trigger again, and the shot fired into the air. Carter tightened his grip, twisting the man's wrist nearly backward. Otto bellowed in pain, his fingers falling open, releasing the gun. The gun fell to the ground at their feet, and Carter kicked it away with his boot, sending it skittering across the dirt.

"Dammit, you're not going to get away with this," Carter said between clenched teeth.

"You should have stayed in jail," the sheriff spat.

The reminder of his last five years of misery, of being locked up while his life passed him by, made Carter's anger mount, and he slammed his fist into Otto's jaw. The man's head snapped back, then Carter shoved him to the ground. They rolled and fought, grunting and trading blows, dust and dirt flying as they hit each other over and over.

Otto grabbed a rock from the ground and swung the jagged point against Carter's temple, the edge connecting an inch below his eyes. Blood spurted and he rocked back, dizzy from the force. Then Otto punched him in the gut again, and he grunted, desperate not to pass out.

Sadie yelled his name, fueling his need to protect her. She had suffered too much already. She needed him now.

He would not let this bastard kill her.

Channeling all his energy and rage into striking back, he swung his fist and connected with

Otto's stomach. The man doubled over with a groan, and Carter took advantage to punch Otto in the ribs. The sound of bones cracking was his reward, and he hit him again, this time so hard the blow knocked the sheriff to the ground.

Otto was a big guy, but his gut and age slowed his reactions, and Carter had had five years of prison fights to hone his skills.

He didn't have to think now. By rote, he used those skills. Otto fought back as Carter pinned him to the ground, but Carter sank his weight onto the man, pinned him with his legs, then punched him in the face, over and over and over.

Five years of rage and brutal beatings with no one to help him drove him to vent his anger. Blood gushed from Otto's nose and mouth, his eyes rolled back in his head, and he moaned in pain, his body going limp as he lost consciousness.

All the nights in that cell, the isolation and despair flashed back, and Carter wanted to punish Otto. He wanted him dead.

So he hit him again and again, smiling as blood pooled from Otto's nose.

But Sadie's soft cry broke through the haze of his rage.

"Carter, stop," she pleaded. "Please, stop, you don't want to kill him."

"Yes, I do." Carter threw another blow.

"No, you don't." Sadie tugged at his arm. "If you do, you'll go back to jail and we'll never clear your name."

Through the haze of his rage, her words registered.

Five years ago he'd been out of control, and he'd ended up in jail.

"We have proof, evidence," Sadie said. "We have the will, and I'll testify, and finally you'll be free."

She gripped his face, and forced him to look at her. "That's what you want, Carter. To be free. And this is not the way to get it."

Carter's vision was blurred, but through the fog, he looked into Sadie's eyes. Her beautiful, dark eyes that he had lost himself in the first time he'd met her.

She was right. Killing Otto would feel good for a few minutes, but then he'd go back to jail and his life would be over. Again.

Not that his future held much hope, but at least if he cleared his name, he wouldn't live his days in a cell waiting to die.

Slowly he climbed off of Otto, then grabbed the sheriff's handcuffs from his belt, rolled the man over and cuffed his hands behind his back.

Sadie had given him a reason to live and to keep fighting for that freedom. And he intended to fight.

SADIE WAS TREMBLING as she searched Carter's face. But she felt blood on his abdomen, and fear mingled with relief. Carter had subdued the sheriff and hadn't killed him, but he was still injured.

"You're bleeding again, Carter. Did he shoot you?"

Carter shook his head, glanced down at his belly and frowned. "No, he just opened up the wound."

"Thank God," Sadie said. "But we need to stop the bleeding."

"Let me call Johnny before Otto comes to."

Sadie nodded and ran to the truck to grab an extra T-shirt to soak up the blood. When she returned, Carter was talking on the phone.

"Yeah, Johnny. We're okay, and Otto's cuffed but he's alive." A pause and Sadie came to him, then began unbuttoning his shirt.

"Thanks, Johnny. We'll be here waiting."

He disconnected the call, and Sadie gripped his arm. "Come on and sit down, Carter. Let me look at the wound."

The sheriff groaned slightly and tried to open his eyes, but he was too weak and passed back out. Sadie balled the shirt into a compress and pressed it against Carter's abdomen, soaking up the blood. Her heart hammered frantically at the feel of his skin beneath her fingers.

They had made love only a little while ago. Then they had almost died.

Although she had told Carter she loved him, he hadn't confessed his love. In fact, he hadn't responded at all.

Except to pull away.

What would happen once the police arrived? Once he was finally free?

Would it be over between them?

CARTER WRESTLED with frustration and despair as they waited on Johnny and the police. The instinct to run was so strong he considered asking Sadie to jump in the truck and suggest they drive to Mexico.

But he was so close to justice he could practically taste it. And he couldn't leave without making sure Otto paid.

Besides, now his father was gone, *if* he cleared his name, this property should revert to him. Unless his father had stipulated otherwise.

"Carter, are you all right?" Sadie asked softly.

He looked into her endless brown eyes, and felt a ghost of a smile tugging at his lips, a confession of his love on the tip of his tongue. Yet too many doubts plagued him to speak. He had stared at prison walls for so long that he hadn't dared to dream what would happen if he was finally exonerated.

A siren wailed in the distance, and he tensed, knowing the police were coming for him. That he wasn't free yet.

He had too much explaining to do. He had broken out of jail. The police still believed he'd injured that guard in the escape. And he was wanted for other murders. Loretta Swinson, Jeff Lester and now his alleged cousin, Elmore Clement. There was also the stolen car.

He was a long way from freedom. And if the police didn't buy the evidence he'd found and Otto somehow beat the charges, he might never be again.

The siren grew louder, then a trail of cars—a police car, an ambulance, then Johnny's truck—rolled over the horizon. Sadie moved up beside him and clutched his arm.

He wanted to assure her everything would be all right, but he'd been railroaded before, and he'd lost his faith.

Then the sheriff's car screeched to a stop, and a tall, lumbering man in uniform climbed out and strode toward him, his gun drawn. A second man with blondish hair in a deputy's uniform followed, swinging his baton as if he was ready to club them at any moment.

Johnny was on his heels, along with a team of paramedics, but the sheriff gestured for them to wait with a raised hand.

"Carter Flagstone," the sheriff said. "I'm Sheriff McRae. You called to turn yourself in?"

Carter cleared his throat. "Yes. This man, Sheriff Otto, tried to kill us. He's also responsible for murdering my father, Loretta Swinson, Jeff Lester—"

"Put down your weapon," the sheriff ordered. "Do it slowly."

"Wait," Sadie cried. "He needs medical attention."

"We'll see he gets it," Sheriff McRae said.

Carter reached for the gun at his waist, then eased it to the ground.

Sheriff McRae retrieved the weapon and jammed it in his belt. "Turn around and put your hands behind your back."

Carter grimaced but did as he said. It was either that or get shot.

He'd known it would be hard to convince the cops to listen to his story. But still, his chest constricted as the sheriff reached for his handcuffs and snapped them around his wrists.

When he'd secured them, the deputy turned to

Sadie. "Sadie Whitefeather, you are under arrest for aiding and abetting an escaped felon and conspiracy to commit murder."

"What?" Carter jerked toward the sheriff, but he yanked his arm to force him to be still.

Then his deputy grabbed Sadie, spun her around and snapped handcuffs on her wrists.

"We'll work this out, Carter," Johnny said. "I'll hire you both a lawyer. This time the truth will come out."

Carter wanted to believe him, but the system had failed him once before. And this time, he'd racked up a series of charges.

If it failed this time, he'd never get out.

Then he looked at Sadie and grimaced. If he had to, he'd make a deal just so she could go free.

Chapter Seventeen

Carter endured the police ride in bitter silence, angry that the sheriff had insisted on a separate car for Sadie. Apparently he didn't want them to have time to collaborate on their story. He obviously believed that if he separated them, he could convince Sadie to turn on him and cut a deal for herself.

He hoped to hell she took it.

She'd been through too much already to have to suffer jail. Especially for a loser like him.

But they took him to the local joint anyway. The paramedics treated him there, then the police hauled him back to the state prison.

This time he was forced into a cell alone, solitary confinement, a punishment and a precaution in case he tried to escape again. The cell air seemed even more stifling than he remembered, the cell smaller, the loneliness so painful that his throat and chest ached.

Just hours before he'd been on the BBL watching the boys grooming horses, breathing in the air and feeling alive. Hoping to have a future that included giving back to the kids there because it felt like the home he'd never had.

And he had held Sadie in his arms and made love to her.

He wanted to hold her and love her again.

Would he ever have the chance?

He laid on his back and counted the cracks in the ceiling, the dust motes floating in the shadows of the hazy darkness, the sounds of prison guards walking, cell keys jangling from their belts, of violence and sex echoing from the chambers deeper within the prison.

He closed his eyes and tried to imagine himself back at the BBL. Living in a cabin and working with the kids and horses. Having a family with Sadie. The life he'd dreamed of years ago.

Finally exhaustion from the fight and his weakened condition claimed him, and he fell into a tormented sleep.

But he jerked awake sometime later, the haunting image of a prison guard leading him to the death chamber vivid in his mind.

He tried to grasp on to the hope he'd felt when he'd called Johnny and decided to turn himself in, but once again hope had a harsh way of dying inside prison walls.

SADIE PACED THE CELL, grateful when morning finally came. She'd spent all night rubbing her prayer beads and meditating, desperate to hold on to her faith.

This time justice would prevail.

It had to. Carter could not stay in prison for a crime he hadn't committed.

Dawn streaked the cellblock through the tiny windows at the top, the sound of prisoners being called to meet with their attorneys or to be escorted to court adding to her nerves. Minutes ticked into hours, and she still hadn't been granted her phone call.

But finally a guard appeared, his face pinched. "Your attorney's here."

"What?" What attorney?

The keys jangled as he unlocked the cell and took her arm. "Follow me. He's waiting for you."

Sadie decided not to question him, but to follow and see what was going on. Maybe Jimmy had discovered her arrest and hired a lawyer for her.

But when she stepped into the interview room, Carter's friend Johnny stood by the door, and an older man with silver at his temples and wire-rimmed glasses had parked himself at the table in the middle of the room.

"Miss Whitefeather," Johnny said. "This is Harper Fitzgerald, your attorney."

"You hired him for me?" Sadie asked, shocked.

"Yes, for you and Carter." Johnny gestured for her to sit. "I've explained the circumstances, but I need you to tell Mr. Fitzgerald your story so he can arrange to have the charges against you dropped."

Sadie's heart stuttered. "Thank you, Johnny. But what about Carter? He's not a murderer, he's a hero. By exposing Otto and this mining venture, he's saving lives on the reservation and the BBL. And who knows how many more if the mining company's methods aren't monitored."

"We're working on getting him a hearing," Johnny said. "First we need your side of the story for the police records." He offered her a tentative smile.

Sadie slid into the chair. "All right."

She carefully relayed every detail of what had happened to her, starting from the threats Lester had made, the attack and his stalking tactics, to she and Carter finding Loretta Swinson's body and then Clement's body, and the evidence they'd found regarding Carter's father's ranch, then Sheriff Otto's attempt to murder them.

When she finished, Johnny gave her an encouraging look, and the lawyer patted her hand. Then he stood and left the room for a moment, and returned later with Sheriff McRae.

"You have to hear this, Sheriff," Mr. Fitzgerald told the sheriff. Then he turned to her. "Sadie, you need to repeat everything you just told me."

Sadie massaged her temple where a headache pulsed. She hadn't slept a wink the night before and wasn't sure she would sleep until she saw Carter again. No telling what could be happening to him in prison. If Otto had been working with someone else, Carter might still be in danger.

So she retold her story, answering the questions the sheriff tossed at her with honesty and ease. No longer did the memory of Lester's hands and knife torment her.

Only the fear that she might never see Carter again did.

CARTER STRUGGLED TO HOLD ON to faith, but he was remanded without bail, so he began counting the days in the cell. The lawyer Johnny had hired had offered him encouragement, and Johnny's detective was working on digging up evidence to corroborate his story.

Sadie had been released, thank God, and she'd asked to visit him, but he had refused. He didn't want her to see him locked away like an animal.

Johnny had informed him that she was staying at the BBL and had been helping out by setting up a clinic for medical purposes. He should have known his friends would come through and take care of her. And she would be wonderful with the boys on the BBL.

Besides, it was time he faced facts and stop clinging to the ridiculous idea that they might have a future. He had nothing to offer.

And she deserved better, especially after all she'd suffered because of him.

Ten days into his incarceration, and he received word that a hearing had been set. Nerves balled in his stomach as he showered and dressed that morning. Brandon had sent him decent jeans and a dress shirt, and he'd shaved for the occasion, wondering if he was ever going to see the daylight without bars blocking the view.

He had been interrogated several times already, and questioned repeatedly to see if he had information about the whereabouts of the other escaped prisoners. He didn't, but he wasn't convinced the police believed him.

Outside the courtroom, his attorney shook his hand, and when he led him inside, the first faces he spotted were Johnny's and Brandon's. Fitzgerald had explained that they had split his retainer, and Carter vowed to pay them back some day.

That is, if he was ever released and got a job. Without freedom, he had no hope of doing either.

Johnny offered him a smile and Brandon gave

him a thumbs-up. Kim was beside him, her support evident in her eyes.

The bailiff called the hearing to order, then the legal jargon spilled out. Finally, after the prosecutor detailed the charges against him, his lawyer took the stage.

"Your Honor, we have evidence to submit today that proves without a doubt that my client Carter Flagstone was not only innocent of the crime he was convicted of five years ago, but barring escaping prison, which was a desperate act on his behalf to prove his innocence, that he was framed for murder and is innocent of all the charges against him."

Carter remained stoic, sitting stone still as Fitzgerald presented his case. Evidence of a money trail from Sheriff Otto to Jeff Lester and Elmore Clement, both former prisoners whom he had coerced into helping him orchestrate his crime, proved a connection. Johnny's detective had uncovered Carter's father's real will, and had proof from a handwriting analyst that Clement had forged the papers giving him ownership of the property, and they produced signed affidavits from Mulligan stating that he had expressed interest in the uranium mines on the Flagstone ranch, land he believed legally belonged to Clement.

Bullet casings from Otto's weapon matched ballistics found in Lester and Clement's body.

A nurse from the local hospital testified regarding the injured guard's condition. "Amos Herbert has been in a coma for the past few days due to injuries sustained during the prison attack. He is now stable and regained consciousness yesterday."

"Was he questioned regarding the attack?" Fitzgerald asked.

The woman nodded, then gave Carter an encouraging smile. "He stated that Mr. Flagstone was not the man who assaulted him, that he actually pulled the other prisoner off of him and saved his life."

The prosecutor jumped up to object. "This is hearsay, Your Honor—"

"It is not hearsay," Fitzgerald stated. "Officer Turner is here to verify this woman's testimony."

"Objection overruled, counselor," the judge said. "Continue, Mr. Fitzgerald."

Fitzgerald called the policeman who corroborated the nurse's story, then Fitzgerald called his last witness.

Carter clenched the table edge as Sadie entered and took the stand.

The bailiff swore her in, and Sadie squared her shoulders and relayed her side of the story.

Carter stared at her in utter awe. She was the

most beautiful and strongest woman he'd ever known. He loved her so much his throat hurt.

And when she stepped down from the stand and looked at him with those enormous brown eyes, he wanted to beg her forgiveness, declare his love, and promise her that he would make everything all right.

The bailiff called a ten-minute recess, and Carter sweated the entire time, unable to look at Sadie or his friends for fear he'd let them down.

Finally the judge returned, his sharp gaze cutting toward Carter. Carter swallowed hard, straining to contain his nerves.

"Under the circumstances and in light of the evidence and testimony I've seen and heard today, I have to rule in the defendant's favor. Mr. Flagstone, you are hereby exonerated, with the court's apology, of course. Every effort will be made to ensure your name is cleared in the community and to instigate monetary retribution for your suffering. You are hereby free to go." He slammed the gavel. "This court is adjourned."

Carter sat in stunned silence, the judge's words echoing over and over in his head. He was free. Exonerated. His name would finally be cleared, the shame of being called a murderer lifted.

Johnny and Brandon whooped with joy, and Kim hugged him. His lawyer patted him on the back and said something about receiving restitution and working on handling his father's will, but Carter barely heard a word.

Sadie was the one he wanted to be with right now.

He looked over at her, the yearning so strong he could barely contain himself.

He could go to her and declare his love. He had his dream. His life back.

Then reality interceded.

No—not all of his dreams.

He was five years behind and broke.

And he couldn't make promises to her when he had nothing to offer.

He was a hard-luck cowboy who had to focus on climbing back into the saddle and overcoming all he'd lost.

Sadie deserved more.

So when Johnny and Brandon dragged him out of the courtroom to celebrate, he gave her an apologetic look, turned and walked away.

SADIE'S HEART BROKE as she watched Carter leave with his friends. She was elated that he had finally been exonerated and was free, but she loved him and wanted to leave the courtroom with him.

Obviously that wasn't Carter's plan.

He had hunted her down to force her to help

him, not because he cared about her, and now he was finished with her.

She sucked in her pride and exited the building. The hot Texas summer sun beat down on her, the sky a crystal-clear blue with powdery soft clouds dotting the distance.

But she felt dismal inside, as if she'd just lost the most important person in her life.

Across the way, she spotted Carter climbing into the cab of a truck with his best friends.

She would not beg for a man's love. And she would always be thankful that Carter had forgiven her for betraying him. And for helping her overcome her fear of being with a man.

Not that she intended to get involved with another man anytime soon.

Maybe never…

No, instead she would reclaim her life just as Carter was about to do. The first step was to look into medical school again and start the application process.

Taking care of the boys at the BBL had reminded her how much she'd wanted to be a doctor.

With the revelations about the uranium mines, there were bound to be more cases of cancer to treat on the reservation. There would also be lawsuits as well, and she would fight for her people. Maybe she would even start a free clinic on the reservation. She would move back there tonight. She couldn't live on the BBL with Carter there and not be able to be with him.

She reached the bottom of the steps and headed toward the parking lot when the truck carrying Carter and his friends drove by. Carter's gaze met hers through the window and for a heartbeat she thought she saw love and yearning flash in his eyes.

Then he frowned and threw up his hand and waved goodbye.

She raised her hand to say the same, then blinked back tears as he disappeared out of sight.

Chapter Eighteen

Four months later

Carter ended the riding session with the ten-year-olds, his heart tugging. Working with the boys at the BBL since his release had helped him heal. He finally felt as if he was making a difference.

He kicked dirt off his boots, then drove to the bar to meet his buddies. Ten minutes later, he accepted the mug of beer from Brandon, then he and Johnny and Brandon clinked glasses.

"Congratulations, buddy," Johnny said. "First you receive retribution from the government for false imprisonment."

Carter smiled, his head still reeling from the meeting with Fitzgerald yesterday. The restitution would have taken years, but his lawyer had cut a deal. Still, it had been far more than he'd expected.

"And you get your old man's land," Brandon said with a hefty sip from his mug.

Johnny patted him on the back. "And now you've sold it and have a fortune."

Carter turned the mug up and drank, overcome with all that had happened the last few weeks. Mulligan had claimed innocence regarding the murders, but faced with numerous lawsuits, stepped down from the Uranium Mining Venture. Carter had imagined freedom but never that he'd come out financially so far ahead. And he'd managed to sell his land to a man who'd taken over the Uranium Mining Venture and signed paperwork agreeing to institute environmental safety standards.

He wanted that for Sadie and her people and the BBL. He'd come to respect and admire all the men involved with the BBL, along with the ranch hands and counselors, and he loved working with the kids.

Brandon rocked back on the back legs of the chair. "So what are you going to do with all that money, Carter?"

Carter shrugged. He'd been happy at the BBL, but still something was missing. "All I ever wanted was my own spread like you guys have."

Johnny and Brandon exchanged smiles, and Carter wondered what the hell they were up to.

"What do you two have up your sleeve?" Carter asked.

Johnny tossed a peanut in the air and caught it in his mouth. "We just happen to know of some ranch land for sale. Rich Copeland, the guy who owns the land next to the BBL, is finally moving."

"Yeah, he's complained ever since we started the BBL and finally decided to give it up," Brandon added.

Next to the BBL? It sounded too good to be true.

Johnny grinned sheepishly. "We also know where you can purchase some start-up horses and cattle."

Carter's chest swelled. The only thing better than being free and having money was having his best friends back. "Sounds like I need to take a look at it."

"We can ride out there later," Brandon told him.

Carter nodded. "You know, I've been thinking."

"About what?" Johnny arched a brow. "Sadie Whitefeather?"

Carter's gut churned. Hell, not a minute went by *without* him thinking about her. "About the BBL. I'd like to be a permanent part of it. Help you grow it."

The chair legs hit the floor as Brandon rocked back down. "We could use a cowboy like you."

"Yeah," Johnny said gruffly. "So far, you've inspired some of the boys not to give up hope, that you can overcome adversity and have a future. You just have to want it bad enough to fight for it."

Another twinge pulled at Carter's gut. He'd thought having freedom, money, a ranch of his own—that it would all be worth it. That it was all he wanted and needed.

But even thinking about buying Copeland's land wasn't as thrilling as he'd expected.

Something else was missing.

Sadie.

Hell, he knew it was Sadie.

But for some reason, he'd been too damn stubborn to admit it.

Johnny's simple silver wedding band and Brandon's gold one—bands he once would have thought looked like nooses around their fingers—reminded him that they both had someone special in their lives. Someone to love.

Someone who loved them.

Sadie had said she loved him.

Had she meant it?

"You're awfully quiet for a celebration," Johnny said.

Carter looked up at his buddies and once again thought how grateful he was to have their friendship. They had wasted so much time being angry.

He didn't want to waste a minute now.

"I have been thinking about Sadie," he said quietly.

Johnny and Brandon exchanged another look. "What are you waiting for?" Johnny asked.

Brandon elbowed him. "Yeah, man, why don't you go after her?"

Carter grimaced, his old insecurities screaming in his head. The bitter things his old man had said. That he was worthless and didn't deserve love. The beatings at the prison. The time running from the law.

The ugliness was all part of him now.

Carter cleared his throat. "I…don't deserve her," he finally admitted.

"Don't start that bull," Brandon growled.

A tense silence descended for a minute, then Johnny cleared his throat. "Yeah, you *do* deserve her," he said quietly.

Brandon poured him another beer. "You just have to believe it."

"But what if it's too late?" What if she'd gone back to the reservation and married Jimmy?

Johnny patted his back. "Then you fight for her just like you have everything else in your life."

Brandon raised his glass for another toast. "Here's to never giving up."

Carter raised his glass and clinked it with his buddies. They were right.

Dammit, Sadie was the best thing that had ever happened to him.

And he was going after her.

SADIE STARED AT THE POSITIVE line on the pregnancy test and smiled, then glanced at the medical school acceptance letter and frowned.

She should be excited over both occasions.

But how would she pay for medical school *and* support a baby?

Taking a deep breath, she pushed to her feet to make a cup of herbal tea, her determination kicking in. She had survived Lester's attack, and she and Carter had overcome huge obstacles to free both of them from the past.

She could raise this child on her own and attend medical school and become a doctor. The people at the reservation needed her.

And thanks to Carter, the water issue was settled. He might not have loved her, but when he'd sold his father's ranch, he'd exposed the problems and convinced the company leader to enforce environmental safety precautions. She would never forget that good deed.

She pressed a hand over the small bump in her belly, an image of Carter's face flashing in her mind. She hoped this baby looked just like him.

But sadness welled inside her that this little boy or girl would never know their daddy.

She had considered calling him and telling him. But Carter had made no move to see her in the past few months, and she refused to trap a man into marriage.

She sipped her tea and looked out at the reservation—the rolling flatland, the scrub brush, the hogans, the prayer teepee, the wild horses roaming in the hills—and felt a peacefulness inside her.

She hoped Carter felt that peace, as well.

The sun was rising higher, blazing hot, so she showered quickly, braided her hair, then dressed in a loose Indian dress, and headed over to the clinic to work with the children. Starting a clinic had been her pet project the first month she'd returned.

This was her future now. The reservation. The children. And soon she would add a little baby of her own.

He or she would be born before the first semester of medical school started. Then again, she could postpone school another year until the baby was older and she could save some money.

It wouldn't be easy, but she would do it. And she would love this child with all her heart, just as she loved its father.

CARTER HAD BEEN TO the Sawdust Saloon looking for Sadie, then to her old apartment, but both the owner of the bar and the apartment complex said she hadn't returned after the hearing.

Amber, one of the waitresses at the saloon, had told him Sadie had moved back to the reservation.

Carter pulled up to the sign marking the entrance, stopped and stared at it, his stomach in knots. Had Sadie reunited with Jimmy?

Hell, it had been four months. She might be married for all he knew.

He might be on the verge of making a fool out of himself.

And Carter didn't like being the fool.

He shifted gears and started to turn the car around, but a falcon flew above, free, its wings fluttering, just as the wild horses ran free in the distance. He was free now.

Free to choose to be alone or to spend his life with the woman he loved and wanted.

He just hoped to hell he wasn't too late.

Then he spotted a little girl about five with a long black braid dangling down her back standing near a building marked Medical Clinic. A building that hadn't been there before. He instinctively knew Sadie had something do with it, and pride filled him.

Then his gaze locked with the little girl's. Her big brown eyes reminded him so much of Sadie that for a moment he couldn't breathe. He imagined what his and Sadie's own child might look like, a daughter or a son, and his heart swelled with love.

Then suddenly the little girl turned and ran back toward the clinic.

Was the little girl a sign?

Not that he believed in signs…

Still, he'd come this far. He couldn't go back and tell Johnny and Brandon that he had chickened out. And he couldn't let his fears imprison him.

So he started the truck again and drove onto the reservation.

Seconds later, he spotted Jimmy outside on the porch of the clinic handing a baby over to its mother.

Perspiration beaded on his skin. Jimmy was a good guy. A damn saint. The type of honest, hard-working, dedicated man Sadie deserved.

For God's sake, the man had even helped *him*. Of course, he'd only done that out of devotion to Sadie.

But dammit, *he* wanted her.

Cursing himself for taking so long to come after her, he parked in front of the clinic and climbed out, then strode up to the porch steps. Jimmy spotted him and raised his hand to shade his eyes from the blinding sun.

"I see you finally showed up," Jimmy said, derision lacing his voice.

Carter tensed. "Yeah. I had some things to take care of."

"Things more important than Sadie?" This time Jimmy's anger resonated loud and clear.

Carter shifted. "No…but I needed time."

Jimmy glared at him. "You don't deserve her."

The man's words echoed the trash-talking his father had done to him for years, and fueled Carter's temper. The temptation to slug him ripped through him, but Carter had vowed to change, to not act like his old man, and clenched his hands by his sides.

"I guess we'll let Sadie decide."

"Let Sadie decide what?"

Carter's breath stalled in his chest when he saw her standing in the door frame, the little girl he'd seen on the street beside her. The little girl waved at him then smiled a gap-toothed smile, giving him courage.

Carter shuffled nervously. "Sadie, is there some place we can go and talk?"

Pain flashed in her eyes for just a moment, but she nodded, then started past Jimmy. "I'll be back—"

He caught her arm. "Call me if you need me."

Sadie offered Jimmy a quick smile, then brushed

past him and they walked down the path leading away from the clinic. But when she turned to study him, his nerves spiked as if a fever raged inside him.

He'd never been so damn scared in his life. Not even when he and Sadie had been trapped in that mine.

Finally they reached a small wooden cabin, and she gestured toward the porch. He settled in the porch swing, and she slipped inside and returned a minute later with a glass of lemonade for both of them.

"Thanks." He turned it up and drank as if he hadn't had water in days.

"What are you doing here, Carter?"

Her soft voice made him jerk his head up. The sun painted a halo of golden light around her, framing her beautiful face. Not for the first time, he thought she looked like an angel.

Knowing if he stalled, he'd probably chicken out and run, then he'd hate himself for doing so, he dropped to one knee in front of her. His hands shook as he removed the velvet ring box from his pocket, flipped it open and held it out toward her. "I love you, Sadie. I…don't know what took me so long to say it except I was a fool, and I didn't think I deserved you, but I love you and I want you to marry me."

For a moment, Sadie simply stared at him as if she was stunned, a soft smile of hope lighting her eyes. A second later, her smile faded, she burst into tears and ran inside the house, the screen door slapping behind her.

Hell. Carter staggered back, shocked. He'd worried that she and Jimmy were involved.

Maybe they were and he *was* too damn late.

No, he couldn't be. Sadie was too important. Dammit, he'd never loved anyone like he loved her.

He vaulted up and rushed inside, slamming the screened door, but he hesitated at the sight of her standing by the window looking out at the wild horses running in the distance. Her shoulders were shaking, and she was crying softly.

"Sadie?" Terrified that he'd lost her or that something was terribly wrong, he inched toward her. "Sadie, what's wrong?" he asked quietly. "If I hurt you, I'm sorry."

She spun around, her eyes red-rimmed and haunted. "Jimmy called you, didn't he? He told you to come here and do this."

"What?" He narrowed his eyes, confused. "Hell, no. He's in love with you and hates my guts. Why would he call me?"

Sadie sniffled. "He really didn't call you?"

Carter shook his head. "No."

"So you don't know…he didn't tell you—"

"Tell me *what?*" Worry clawed at him. Was she sick or something?

His lungs ached for a breath as he closed the distance between them and captured her hands in his own. "What is it? Talk to me." Panic seized him. "I should have come sooner, but I was confused and scared and I wanted to get my life together."

"Oh, Carter." Suddenly a small smile softened her mouth, confusing him even more. Then she released his hand and pressed one hand over her stomach.

"What?" Carter rasped. For God's sake, he was going to faint. "Please, you're killing me. Tell me what's wrong."

"Jimmy didn't tell you about the baby?" she whispered.

"Baby?" Carter's legs buckled. Sadie caught him and helped him to the sofa.

Sadie laughed softly, then knelt beside him. "Yes, when you proposed, I thought you knew, that that was the only reason you asked me to marry you."

He shook his head, the shock turning to joy and excitement. "No, my God, no. Sadie, I…love you." He dropped down to the floor beside her. "I've missed you so much, but at first I didn't have anything to offer you. No money. No place to live. I had no way to take care of you."

"You did take care of me, Carter. And I never wanted money," Sadie said. "All I wanted was you."

Carter realized he'd been an idiot. But he intended to make up for it. He cupped her face between his hands. "And all I want is you."

Sadie licked her lips, her eyes moist. "But it's not just me now, Carter. We're going to have a son or a daughter."

Fear that he would be like his father slammed into Carter.

But the trust and love shining in her eyes made his doubts quickly fade. He would never be like his old man.

"I know, and I love you, Sadie." He kissed her deeply, then lowered his head and kissed her belly. "And I will love our baby and be the best father I can be to him."

"Or her," Sadie said with a laugh.

He kissed her again, then framed her face with his hands. "I have some things to tell you. I bought a ranch. It's next to the BBL and I'm volunteering there—"

"That's wonderful," Sadie said. "And I was accepted into medical school."

Carter picked her up and swung her around, and

she squealed with joy. "Now, *that's* something to celebrate."

Sadie looped her arms around his neck. "No, marrying you is something to celebrate."

Carter nodded, then they kissed frantically. One kiss led to another, and they fell on the bed together, touching and stroking, and laughing.

Then Carter slowly undressed her.

And as he joined his body with hers, he realized Sadie had given him the one thing that money couldn't buy—well, two things.

Her love and a baby.

* * * * *